A Prayer for the Night

D0168704

Other Ohio Amish Mysteries by P. L. Gaus:

Blood of the Prodigal

Broken English

Clouds without Rain

Cast a Blue Shadow

A PRAYER for the NIGHT

AN OHIO AMISH MYSTERY

P. L. Gaus

Ohio University Press
Athens

Avon Lake Public Library
32649 Electric Blvd.
Avon Lake, Ohio 44012

Ohio University Press, Athens, Ohio 45701
www.ohio.edu/oupress
© 2006 by Paul L. Gaus

Printed in the United States of America

All rights reserved

Ohio University Press books are printed on acid-free paper ∞ ™

14 13 12 11 10 09 08 07 06   5 4 3 2 1

Library of Congress Cataloging-in-Publication Data
Gaus, Paul L.
   A prayer for the night : an Ohio Amish mystery / P.L. Gaus.
      p. cm.
   ISBN-13: 978-0-8214-1672-3 (cloth : alk. paper)
   ISBN-10: 0-8214-1672-3 (cloth : alk. paper)
   ISBN-13: 978-0-8214-1673-0 (pbk. : alk. paper)
   ISBN-10: 0-8214-1673-1 (pbk. : alk. paper)
      1. Amish Country (Ohio)—Fiction. 2. Amish youth—Crimes against
—Fiction. 3. Branden, Michael (Fictitious character)—Fiction.
4. College teachers—Fiction. 5. Amish—Fiction. I. Title.
PS3557.A9517P73 2006
813'.54—dc22

2005036053

Avon Lake Public Library
32649 Electric Blvd.
Avon Lake, Ohio 44012

For the women—Madonna, Laura, and Amy

Preface

ALL of the characters in this novel are purely fictional, and any apparent resemblance to people living or dead is entirely coincidental. The Holmes County setting for this story is authentic, but Millersburg College is fictional. The GPS coordinates for Gypsy Springs School are accurate. The practice of Rumschpringe is authentic, though rarely carried to the extremes depicted here.

In the vicinity of Saltillo, straddling Township Lane 129, there is a tree farm owned by Dick and Carol Potts. In the area, there are also two abandoned mines where Amish still chip out blocks of coal. Also, there are several old cabins used formerly by the city of Mansfield for summer camps for underprivileged and at-risk children. Near a spot that used to be marked by an old tree with an elbow-shaped trunk, there is a cave entrance that leads to a larger cavern, with a second opening to light, some hundred yards uphill from the bottom. The story is told that a log cabin was built over the upper portal of the cave, and that settlers could escape into the old cave when attacked by Indians.

The wedding ceremony depicted here has been adapted from the translation of an authentic ceremony provided by the late William I. Schreiber in his important book *Our Amish Neighbors,* which is still available from his estate through the Florence O. Wilson bookstore on the campus of the College of Wooster, in Wooster, Ohio.

The author wishes to thank Ohio University Press director David Sanders and editor Nancy Basmajian for pushing the real story here out into light, as well as the many fine professionals at Ohio University Press. Thanks also to Dick and Carol Potts.

Then we will no longer be infants, tossed back and forth by the waves, and blown here and there by every wind of teaching and by the cunning and craftiness of men in their deceitful scheming.

Ephesians 4:14

FRIDAY, JULY 23

1

Friday, July 23
7:45 A.M.

SARA YODER drove her black buggy in bright sun up to the high ridgeline at Saltillo and stopped the Standardbred horse on the blacktop at the intersection of county roads 407 and 68, southeast of Millersburg. It had been two and a half years since she had entered her wild period, her Rumschpringe, quitting school on her sixteenth birthday. Just a week ago she had crossed this ridge in a red Firebird, heading north for the weekend out of her little Amish valley along Township 110 to the bars in Wooster. Dressed English and running wild. Freed from the everyday constraints of Old Order Amish life by the Rumschpringe.

Her horse was lathered from the climb out of the valley, so she popped her whip in the air and pulled forward into the shade of an oak, thinking that Bishop Raber just might have been right all along. The preachers, too. Life out there with the English was dangerous. The winds of temptation were too strong for anyone. But hadn't the Old Order allowed it? Hadn't she been set free by tradition, to get the wildness out of her system, to see all of the English world she could handle, knowing that soon, at this reckoning point in her life, she'd be asked to make a decision? To turn from the world and come home to a lifetime of Amish obedience? To know full well what was out there among the English and freely decide to turn from that sinfulness and join the Old Order?

But Sara Yoder also knew too much now of what the English had to offer. She knew firsthand what life could be like out there in the world. What the real differences between an Amish and an English life were. And it surprised her that she wasn't at all sure that the English were right. Perhaps it really was all vanity and pride, as her parents had assured her.

Truth be told, Sara wasn't sure about even the small things anymore, much less about the consecrated life her parents expected her to lead. Marry at eighteen, join the Old Order congregation, raise a dozen children, and submerge her identify in conformity. Surrender who she was for the sake of humility. To be the same, act the same, live the same as everyone else. To live only for the community of believers. No longer to be an individual. No longer to be just Sara.

In the English world, Sara Yoder was beginning to like the separate person she was becoming. She liked the choice of clothes, the modern conveniences, the pace and feel of freedom. She liked the vision she had of Sara Yoder separate from everyone else, a unique and distinct personality. Free to act and do as she felt. Free to move, breathe, live in the open. Free to be herself.

In the end, though, the scrap of newsprint she held on her lap gave the lie to all that English freedom. It called her to face the truth about the dangers that were out there in the world. It reminded her that John Schlabaugh and Andy Yoder no longer answered their cell phones or returned text messages. Just when John had promised them all the means to free themselves from the vise grips of backward Amish traditions, he had disappeared. Andy Yoder, too. There wasn't going to be any great emancipation for the John Schlabaugh Rumschpringe gang of Saltillo. There weren't going to be any easy answers. No easy escapes.

Sara cast her eyes to the newspaper clipping and read the cryptic lines in the correspondence section of the *Budget*. Four lines of numbers, demanding attention from the handful of readers who could decipher them, inserted among the scores of family letters from Amish all over the world. The *Sugarcreek Budget*, published each Wednesday, and mailed to anyone, anywhere, who might be interested to know what had happened recently in the lives of the Helmuths in Kansas, or the Peacheys in Ontario. Troyers, Millers, or Yoders. Who had been born, and who had died, in Texas. The quality of the wheat harvest in Mexico that year. Family news from around the world, in an Amish paper published for Amish readers everywhere.

But Sara was concerned only with the four lines of type that were meant, ominously, for her. A greeting number. A location— latitude and longitude. And a salutation number:

3

N 40° 31.174'

W 81° 53.890'

2

Only she and eight others would know what it meant. Anyone in the John Schlabaugh Rumschpringe gang that year. This was their meeting place. This was where they gathered, out of sight of their families, for their running-wild trips to town, once their chores were finished. Once the weekend had come, and they had changed into English clothes. Their parents discreetly looking aside. Pretending not to worry.

Sara folded the paper, set it beside her on the leather seat, and snapped her whip lightly over the withers of her horse. She worked the buggy slowly past the traffic triangle at the top of the ridge and dropped down through the cool shade of the tree farm on the gravel lane of Township 129. At the bottom of the hill, she turned south on County Road 58, crossed Lower Sand Run, and turned eventually onto a narrow, pebbled drive that took her through a stand of pines, around a curve, and up to a small clearing. Near a pond at the edge of a cornfield stood a small red barn. As she pulled to a stop in front of the barn doors, a raccoon with dirty paws scrambled out from under the exterior wall of the barn and scurried off into the corn.

She hitched her horse to a wooden railing that John Schlabaugh had posted in the ground beside the barn, and a rusted, blue Buick

Skyhawk rolled into the clearing. As she tugged the looped reins tight on the railing, Henry Erb climbed out of the little sedan. He was dressed in English clothes—designer jeans, a yellow golf shirt, and white running shoes—but his Dutch-boy haircut gave him away as Amish.

Henry said, "You saw the *Budget,* too?"

Sara nodded and asked, "Have you seen John or Abe?"

"No," said Erb, and glanced around expectantly. "Anybody else been here?"

He saw that the lock on the barn doors was hanging loose, and he came around the front of his car to open the doors.

Sara joined him and said, "I should have come out here yesterday."

"It was just coordinates in the newspaper," Henry said. "What are we supposed to do with that?"

Sara said, "I wouldn't think anything of it if John and Abe weren't missing."

"I tried their cells again this morning," Henry said. "Still nothing."

Sara took the left side and Henry the right, and they swung the heavy wooden doors open. There was a damp and musty odor as they entered the gloom of the barn. Henry reached up to a kerosene lantern hanging on the inside wall, lit the wick, and carried the sooty lamp into the barn. At the far edge of the light, an old, red Pontiac Firebird sat with its stern backed up against the far wall.

Sara followed Henry to the car. He held aloft the light to shine it into the front seat. Sara peered into the passenger-side window, touched the vinyl seat, and brushed off a crusty rust-red residue. She showed her fingers to Erb. "John and Abe must have had another fight," she said. "Right? It doesn't mean anything more."

Erb shrugged with a grimace, and walked around to the driver's side. He opened the door, looked in, and said, "Keys are missing."

Sara said, "Did you ever know John to park his car here?"

Erb frowned. "No. He keeps it out at his trailer. With mine and Jeremiah's." With a clipped, stuttering cadence, Erb added, "John would never leave his car. If he's parked it here, then something's wrong."

"It's gotta be the drugs," Sara said ruefully, backing away from the Pontiac. "They've gotten themselves in too far." She looked furtively around the barn, anxiety showing on her face.

"John's too smart for that," Erb said, closing the car door.

"I'm not so sure," Sara countered. She turned from the car and saw something in the near corner. "Bring the light over here," Sara said, kneeling on the dirt floor of the barn. When Erb brought the light, they could see a ragged hole scratched in the dirt.

"I scared off a raccoon when I drove up," said Sara. The edge of a plastic bag showed in the hole. Sara scooped dirt out from around the bag and pulled it loose.

Inside the bag were a black leather wallet, two car keys on an antique Pontiac fob, a GPS receiver in a plastic camouflage case, and a cell phone. Erb said, "Those are John's keys. For the Firebird."

Sara took out the wallet and thumbed it open. "This is John's wallet, too." She pulled out the GPS receiver and asked with growing dread, "Is this John's GPS unit?"

"Can't tell," Erb said. "John's is like all of ours. I guess it's his."

Puzzled, Sara said, "This is not John Schlabaugh's phone."

"Right," Erb said, "but whose?"

Sara frowned, shook her head, and dropped the items back into the plastic bag.

Erb stepped back toward the doors of the barn and said, "Look, Sara. I don't like it here. John's got some kind of funny business going on, and I don't think we ought to be messing in with it."

Sara asked, "Who put those coordinates in the *Budget*, Henry?"

"I don't know." Backing out the door.

"You need to stay and help me figure this out," Sara insisted.

"I was going up to Wooster. You ought to come along," Erb said sheepishly. He reached his car, got in quickly, cranked the engine to life, and spun around in the dirt to point his Buick back down the lane. With his left arm hanging out the window, he said, "Look, Sara. This is John's business. He calls the shots. So I'm not getting involved."

Sara shook her head, not bothering to hide her mounting consternation. "There's something wrong here, Henry. And none of us is innocent anymore. We need to face this."

"I can't get mixed up in any more of John's schemes. The bishop has been to see my father already."

Sara took her cell phone out of the front pocket of her apron and said, "I know someone who can help."

"I can't stay," Erb said, his voice strained. "I'm going up to Wooster tonight. If you want to go, come down to the schoolhouse. I'm going to get the others to come along."

Sara gave a dissatisfied shake of her head and waved Erb off. She stood in front of the barn doors, punching in the phone number, and watched Henry Erb speed down the lane toward County 58 and disappear into the overhanging pines.

While she waited for the call to go through, Sara held the plastic bag up to her eyes and studied the contents with growing apprehension. The call went dead. She lowered the phone from her ear and saw a "No Signal" indication on the display. She untied the reins, got back into her buggy, trotted her horse up to the higher ground at Saltillo, and tried the call again. With better reception on the ridge, she got Pastor Cal Troyer at his church in Millersburg. She explained where she was and asked him to come out to meet her at the barn. When he asked what her problem was, she gave an evasive answer.

Pressed further, Sara said, "It's two of my friends, Cal. They've been gone for a week now, and I just found one of their cars parked in this little barn. It shouldn't be there. And some of his stuff was buried in the corner."

"I'm with a friend, Sara. OK if I bring him along?" Cal asked.

"Can't you just come out here yourself, Cal?"

"It's someone you can trust, Sara."

Sara hesitated, thinking she shouldn't have called.

Cal said, "Professor Michael Branden, Sara. You know who he is. Teaches history at Millersburg College."

"Is he the one who rescued Jeremiah Miller a few years back?"

"Yes. The Millers know him and his wife Caroline well. They are Amishleiben, Sara."

"Then I guess he can come. But just the two of you, Cal. I don't know what's going on out here. I don't want to get anyone in trouble with the law, but I'm starting to get a little rattled, and I don't like it."

"Maybe you'd better tell me what's going on, Sara."

"When you get here, Cal. I'll tell you what I know."

"OK, but are you still going to come in to the church this afternoon? For our regular talk?"

"I don't know, Cal. Maybe I shouldn't talk with you anymore. Maybe something's gone wrong out here. Right now, I just want you to come out and tell me what you think."

"Can I tell the professor a little bit about what you've told me in the past several weeks?"

"Why?"

"I just think it will help if he knows a little of the background. How you kids are getting along. The Rumschpringe."

"OK, but I'm not sure we've even got a Rumschpringe gang anymore. The group has kind of fallen apart."

"OK, Sara. Tell me how to get there."

2

Friday, July 23
8:50 A.M.

WHEN Cal Troyer and Michael Branden drove up the lane to the barn Sara had described, they found her standing beside her buggy horse, holding a water bucket up to its nose. She saw them coming, put the bucket down, loosened the reins so the horse could reach it, and stepped forward on the dirt patch in front of the barn to greet them.

Cal offered his hand to Sara. She took it lightly, a little shy about it, and found herself reassured by the touch of his callused palm and firm grip. His arms were thick, and muscled with knotty strength from the work he did as a carpenter. The pastor was dressed in jeans and a blue work shirt. His boots were old and scuffed. He introduced the professor, and Branden came forward and shook her hand, too.

The professor was dressed in jeans, loafers, and a light blue cotton shirt with a button-down collar. His brown hair was cut short and parted, a patch of silver showing at his temples. He seemed strong to Sara, and trim. Confident.

Branden judged Sara to be about eighteen years old. She was dressed in a long, plain, dark plum dress with a white lace apron. Despite the gathering heat, she wore black hose and a pair of soft black leather walking shoes. She carried a small, black cloth purse on a thin black loop. Her black hair was gathered in a neat bun, tucked up under a white head covering, and she wore wire-rimmed spectacles, silver in color, over her large brown eyes. Her complexion was a flawless ivory, her cheeks tinged with rose. If he hadn't talked with Cal Troyer on the trip out, Branden might have seen nothing in Sara Yoder but the demure serenity of one of the county's Peaceful Ones. But he now could see that, in spite of her carefully controlled manner, Sara Yoder was more than a little worried.

Sara looked Branden over skeptically and glanced back at Cal. Cal smiled and tilted his head briefly in Branden's direction. Branden held his peace. He shaded his eyes with his hand in the bright morning sun and kept them on Cal.

Cal, no stranger to Amish reserve, said to Branden, "Sara lives with her parents down by Saltillo."

Branden said to the girl, "Then you know Panther Hollow pretty well."

Sara shrugged, rubbed her hands together nervously, and said, "I reckon I've been there a few times. It's a place where kids go."

Cal said, "Sara has been all over, Mike. Holmes County, anyway. Some of the boys in her gang own cars."

"Gang?" Branden asked.

"That's what we call it," Sara said, flustered. "John Schlabaugh's gang out of Saltillo. It's just a band of kids."

Branden held Sara's eyes with his steady gaze, and Sara eventually added, "It's a harmless little group of us. Nine to start with, now just seven, I fear. We kind of run together, is all. It's our parents who can't stand the strain." She shifted self-consciously on her feet, and wandered over to the shade beyond the open barn doors.

Branden followed and said, "Cal tells me you've been having some problems. You've been talking with him a couple of times a week?"

"I've been worried," Sara whispered, and furrowed her brow.

Cal said, "It's probably not as bad as you think, Sara."

"They're about ready to kick me out of the house," Sara blurted.

Cal cleared his throat and said, "Maybe it's not that bad."

"All the younger kids know it, Cal. I can see it in their eyes."

"Maybe they're just worried about you," Cal said. "We've talked about this before."

"Rachel is only four. She came crying to me yesterday, Cal. Wanted to know if I was going away."

"She's your sister?" Branden asked.

"Cousin. It's a close family, Professor. We all live right next to each other on the farm my granddaddy started."

"Why would she think you're going away?" Cal asked.

"Because her parents have talked about me with their kids. Warning them. They are all watching to see which way I'll swing. Stay Amish or go English. They think I'll be lost to them. Now they don't ask me to take care of the little ones anymore."

"They must think you've strayed pretty far," Branden said. His solicitous tone took the sting from his words.

"You wouldn't believe half the stuff I could tell you, Professor," Sara replied. She toed the dirt between the barn doors and seemed troubled to be talking so freely.

"What has happened, Sara?" Cal said.

"The bishop is getting nervous, Cal," Sara said. "I've got maybe a month. He's already been to see Henry Erb's parents about this. But it's John Schlabaugh and Abe Yoder that I'm worried about. John's Firebird is parked in this barn, and it shouldn't be."

Cal held her gaze, thinking there must be more that she wanted to say. She seemed unnerved in a way that he had never seen. In their talks, Sara Yoder had been open and forthright to a surprising degree about her youthful lifestyle. And Cal knew that Sara Yoder was racing up to a crisis point in her life over her Amish heritage. Over the crucial life decisions she would soon be forced to make. So Cal had heard it all in their afternoon talks. Still, in the shade this morning, Sara Yoder seemed more unraveled than he had thought she could be. He smiled, shrugged, and said, "Sara, is there more?"

Sara was silent for a long time, eyes closed to slits, thinking. All the troubles she could bear seemed folded together in her brow.

Eventually, she backed up a bit, blew a little air out through her lips to ease her anxiety, and sighed, "This is a mistake. I'm sorry, Cal, Professor Branden. I shouldn't have bothered you. There's nothing you can help me with."

Branden read her uncertainty and said, "I'd like to be of some help to you, Sara."

Sara said, "I don't think anyone can help us now."

"Give us a chance, Sara," said Cal. "At least tell us what you've found."

Sara raised her arms and let them flop at her sides. She stepped over to her buggy, took a folded scrap of newsprint off the seat, and handed the clipping to the professor. She waited for him to read the short lines of type. "That clipping is from Wednesday's *Sugarcreek Budget*," she said.

Branden read the type a second time and said, "Do you know what it means? Those are coordinates. You know the GPS system?"

"Yes. We've got those GPS units," Sara said. She pulled a receiver out of her purse, waved it briefly, and said, "John Schlabaugh got these GPS receivers for all of us, and matching cell phones for everyone in our group." Embarrassed, she explained, "So we could arrange our little parties."

Branden glanced at Cal, who said, "This group of kids has gone a tad modern, Mike."

Branden nodded and said, "Tell us about those coordinates, Sara."

Sara held her eyes closed a moment, then looked up at Branden and seemed to take his measure. Eventually her eyelids puddled over and she took back the newspaper clipping, folded it several times into a tight square, and slowly put it back in her purse. She studied the professor a moment longer, and then Cal. With a halfhearted smile, she said, "Those coordinates are for this spot here at the barn. Our usual meeting place."

Branden thought about the incongruities in a little band of Amish kids tracking each other with cell phones and GPS receivers.

He waited a beat. "Modern can be a rough way to go, Sara, if you're not prepared for it," he said.

Sara stared at her hands. "Modern looks pretty good when you've grown up backward. At least it does at first."

"I think it'll help if you tell me a little about it," Branden said. "For instance, I suppose there's some drinking at your parties."

"I wish that was all there was," Sara answered.

"How many kids in your group?"

"Like I said, it used to be nine. Big John Schlabaugh's gang out of Saltillo. Now it's only seven. Two girls and five boys."

"Should I have been talking with any of them?" Cal asked.

"None of those boys is going to own up to any of it," Sara said. "The other girl? I don't know for sure what she'd tell you."

"Maybe if you asked them to talk with me or the professor?"

"I'm not going to stick around, Cal," Sara said forcefully. "It's not safe." Her eyes flooded with tears, and she softened quickly. "It's the other kids," she said. "I want you and Cal to help the other kids. Even if they won't talk to you. They just don't understand the danger they're in."

Sara pulled a tissue out of her purse and wiped her eyes. More tears came, and she dried those away, sniffed, and blew her nose. In a voice as soft as a flute she asked, "Why does it all have to be so hard? God's will? I wouldn't know that if it bit me on the . . . Sorry. If it bit me."

"Have you talked with your parents about any of this?" Branden asked.

"Parents these days don't understand anything. I can't believe they ever did."

Branden smiled and waited for Sara to look at him. When she did, he said, "We'll do what we can, Sara. Tell us what you need."

She nodded, dropped her gaze to her hands, and let her shoulders slump with the weight of her burdens. After a spell, she began talking quietly.

"There sits John Schlabaugh's car, and nobody has heard from him in over a week. Abe Yoder, too. Everybody thought John Schlabaugh was such a great leader. So charismatic. He was going to show us all the world. Cars, cities, everything. We were all really going to have a run at it. A lifetime of fun in the span of a couple of years. Live the fast life, the Rumschpringe, before we settle down.

"But John's just not cut out for the important things. He's just a drifter, plain and simple. He's a child, really. He just drifts on the wind.

"And we've gone along with just about everything he could think up. Like there was no tomorrow. Now we're all in trouble, and there's no way out. And it's really big trouble, too. It's got to be why John and Abe are missing. Why John's car is here. He'd never give up his car.

"This isn't the penny-ante stuff Amish kids normally get mixed up in. It's not throwing tomatoes at cars or knocking over mailboxes. It's way bigger than that now, and one of us is going to end up hurt."

Branden watched her intently. He struggled to reconcile the seemingly plain and simple Amish girl he saw before him with the remarkable things she had said. No doubt she would have admitted to none of it if she had not known Cal Troyer so well. As a gentle lead into weightier matters, Branden said, "Let's start with something simple, Sara. Tell me more about those coordinates. Why were they published in the *Budget*?"

Sara fished the paper out of her purse, unfolded it, and handed it back to Branden. "That last number?" she said, apparently relieved to be talking about something practical. "That's Abe Yoder's code. He's 2. I'm the leading 3. We each have a number to sign a message with."

"What is John Schlabaugh's number?" Branden asked.

"He's 1," Sara said.

"Why do you need numbers?" Cal asked. "Doesn't your phone display the name of the person calling you?"

"It's John Schlabaugh again. He likes secret things. He says it's all numbers in the modern world. Phone numbers, house numbers, social security numbers, credit card numbers. So he made me 3. He is 1. Messages are very short. But mostly I think he likes the secrecy. Sometimes he calls from a prepaid cell phone he gets from a guy up in Wooster. He says it's untraceable. So, I get a 1 on my text messages, that's him, and his new cell number is the only text in the message. He sends us all his new phone number each month, when he buys a new phone. Anonymous, prepaid cell phones, because he says the government can't trace them."

Cal asked, "What?"

"John says the government can listen in on the airwaves that cell phones use. So he doesn't want too many people knowing who he is. He's just the number 1."

"What do you think this message means?" Branden asked, drawing her attention back to the newspaper clipping.

"If it came on my phone, it'd mean Abe wants me to meet him at a certain place. Here, at those coordinates. So there's the leading 3, and that stands for me. Then the coordinates, followed by Abe Yoder's 2. Sara Yoder to meet Abe Yoder at those coordinates. John and Abe really go in for that secret message stuff. Trouble is, no one has heard from John for a week. Haven't heard from Abe Yoder, either. They haven't answered their phones, and they haven't replied to our messages. We must have sent a hundred by now."

"Are Abe and John in the habit of making trips out of town, or of not answering their phones?" Branden asked.

Sara shook her head, hesitated, and said, "They run together pretty much all of the time, Abe and John. Mostly they're all over our little valley. Up and down the Doughty Valley, too. Millersburg, Becks Mills, and Charm. They think they own the place because they have cars and a tractor.

"And then there's the fights lately. John's a mean drunk. And Abe's too proud to back down. One of these days they're really going to hurt each other. There's blood on the front seat of the Firebird in there, so they've been fighting again. But they've gotten too big for their britches, I'll tell you that much. Making those secret runs down to Columbus. Like the bishop wasn't going to find out about that."

Branden read the expression on her face and said, "I gather you don't approve of those Columbus runs." He glanced quickly to Cal to see if the pastor had caught special meaning in that. Cal tipped his chin in the smallest nod.

Sara shook her head. "Anyway, I came out here to our meeting place after I read that note in the *Sugarcreek Budget*. Because that message should have been sent by Abe Yoder to my phone instead of to the correspondence section of the *Budget*."

"You think the message is for you?" Branden said.

"Me or someone in our outfit," Sara said. "We're the only ones who could know what it means."

Branden held silence, and looked questioningly to Cal and back steadily at Sara.

Sara shrugged her shoulders and said, "Like I said, John and Abe are missing. And, now, I've found this buried here in the barn."

She reached into her buggy and lifted the plastic bag off the floorboards. She held it up in the sun, and Cal and Branden came forward to inspect the contents. Cal took the bag, fished out each of the items inside, and handed them one at a time to the professor.

Her eyes open wide with alarm, Sara said, "I really didn't know what I'd find out here. A raccoon had dug this bag up from the corner of the barn. And the dirt was all loose in that spot. Not like the packed dirt in the rest of the barn." She glanced at the collection of items Branden held and said, "Those are mostly John Schlabaugh's things, but I don't know about the phone. John doesn't use that kind of phone. But that's his wallet."

Cal took the wallet and pulled out an odd collection of business cards and receipts. Sara said, "John doesn't have a driver's license, if that's what you're looking for. But there ought to be some money. John always had a lot of cash. It's just not right. Something bad has happened."

Cal shook his head and handed the wallet to the professor.

Branden stuck the wallet in his front jeans pocket, flipped open the cell phone, and found the battery dead. To Sara he said, "Where can we charge the phone?"

"In the car, I think," Sara said, and reached out for the keys. She stepped into the barn, opened the door of the red Firebird, sat behind the wheel, and started the engine. Branden handed the phone to her, and she retrieved a car charger from the glove compartment. Efficiently, as if she were glad for the distraction, she plugged the phone into the cigarette lighter and got out, saying, "Those chargers work really fast. We've all got the same models."

Branden said, "I'm going to pull this outside," and got in behind the wheel. He rolled the car out through the sliding doors into the sunlight, and parked it with its nose pointed back down the lane. Sara followed the car out and stood beside the driver's window while Branden opened the phone. After punching a few keys, Branden stretched the charger cord to hold the phone out the window for Sara to see, and asked, "Recognize this number?"

"It's John Schlabaugh's number," Sara said, and glanced back nervously toward the dark interior of the barn.

"That's the last number called on this phone," Branden said. "It was a week ago. Last Friday."

Sara took the phone, keyed it, looked at the display, and said, "This is Abe Yoder's phone. And that was John Schlabaugh's latest number you displayed. So, Abe called John last Friday."

Branden wrote the two numbers down on a little pad he took from the breast pocket of his shirt, set the phone, still connected to the charger, on the dash, and climbed out of the low car, leaving the engine growling.

From the wide doors to the barn, Cal said, "There's more here, Mike."

Branden turned and saw Cal standing just inside the door, with the blade of a shovel balanced on the toe of his work boot. The professor walked over to Cal, a few steps ahead of Sara.

Sara came up behind him and asked, "What more?"

Cal said, "Sara, there's more in the hole than that little plastic bag. But I'm not sure you should be looking at it."

Sara pushed past Cal and went over to the corner, where the pastor had deepened the hole with the shovel. As Cal and the professor came up beside her, tears began to line her cheeks. She had the fingers of both hands wrapped around her throat as if to throttle a scream. A strangled sound droned from inside her, like the low note of a bagpipe. She was backing up from the loosened dirt as if the shallow trench were full of writhing copperheads.

In the opening Cal had cleared of dirt, there was a brown leather work boot and the rolled cuff of a pair of Amish denim trousers. The professor straddled the narrow hole on his knees and pulled up on the boot. There was enough resistance to suggest weight in the trouser leg. He pulled back the cuff of the trousers to reveal white skin and immediately dropped the fabric. Cal gave him a hand up, and Branden brushed off his knees. Through the barn door, they heard an engine rev, and when they ran outside, they saw the red Firebird churning its wheels in the gravel, hurtling down the lane that led out to Holmes County 58.

3

Friday, July 23
9:30 A.M.

BRANDEN darted a few yards down the lane and stopped. In the bright sun, he punched numbers on his cell phone, and got no signal. He shook his head and called back to Cal, "You got anything on yours?"

Cal flipped his phone open, and said, "Nothing. Hills block the signals down in here."

"Where's our best bet around here, Cal?"

"If we run up 129, that will put us up on that high ridge at Saltillo."

"We need to make two calls, Cal. Fast. One to Bruce Robertson down at the jail, and one to Abe Yoder's cell phone in that Pontiac. If she hasn't turned it off."

Cal shaded his eyes and said, "I'll stay back and wait for Robertson. You'll have a signal up in Saltillo, I'm sure of it."

Branden backed his truck around in front of the sliding doors of the barn, shot Cal a look of consternation, and gunned back down the lane to Holmes County 58. He turned right and then right again on Township 129, and raced his light truck up the long, steep gravel road, in deep shade, beside Lower Sand Run, spraying gravel. At the top of the hill, he cranked north onto County 407 and sped into Saltillo, a ridgetop community of less than a dozen homes, a town so peaceful that morning that Branden found it surreal.

Over the high ridge, the sky was a deep and cloudless blue. The hills fell away in layers, receding in fading shades of green to the west. Small Amish children in denim trousers and cotton dresses played, laughing, on a swing set in a yard just downslope from the road. A woman was out hanging splashes of deep Amish colors on a clothesline beside a sturdy brick house.

With the image of a denim cuff in a shallow grave fresh in his mind, Branden parked on the blacktop at the north point of the triangle, got out, and keyed his cell phone. He called Abe Yoder's cell number first, hoping to raise Sara Yoder. The call went through and rang several times, but no one answered. Next, he jabbed out the number of the jail switchboard and got Ellie Troyer-Niell, Robertson's dispatcher-secretary.

When she answered, Branden said, "Ellie, it's Mike Branden. We've found a body."

Ellie said, "Whoa there, Doc. Let me get the sheriff."

Brusquely, Bruce Robertson's voice came over the line. "Where are you, Mike?"

"Saltillo. The body's in a barn off of 58. Cal is down there now. I had to come up the hill to Saltillo to make the call."

"My guys are out there, too," Robertson said. "At old Spits Wallace's place on the north side of 129."

"I just drove by there," Branden said, dabbing with a white handkerchief at the beads of sweat on his forehead.

"There's blood on the kitchen wall out there," Robertson said. "And nobody can remember seeing Wallace for the last week or so."

"Yeah, well, whatever you do, don't let any of your guys go into his house," Branden said.

"They're in the kitchen now," Robertson said.

"Get them out!" Branden barked.

"Good grief, Mike, why?"

"Spits Wallace's house is booby-trapped," Branden shouted. "You're gonna get your people all shot up."

Robertson said, "Ellie," and Branden heard Ellie in the background, saying, "Already on it, Bruce."

"How do you know anything about booby traps?" Robertson asked Branden over the speaker phone.

"Don't you remember those stories I used to tell you when we were kids? About the old guy who collected gold coins?"

"Yeah?" Robertson said, sounding skeptical.

"That was Spits Wallace's father, old Earl Wallace. The house was booby-trapped then, and I'd bet it still is."

"Why?"

"Because old man Wallace had about a million bucks' worth of old gold coins stuffed into dozens of canvas moneybags under the furniture. Didn't trust the banks."

"Like I said, I've got blood splatter on Wallace's kitchen wall," Robertson growled. "There's also blood smeared on the linoleum. Is that gonna be from one of his booby traps?"

"Can't say, but he's got something rigged in nearly every room. Down in the basement, too. Don't let your guys back in that house until I can make it down there. His daddy, old Earl, showed me once where the traps were. Maybe they're still the same."

Ellie came over the phone, saying, "I've relayed that message to Ricky, Professor. He's pulling his men out of the house now."

"OK," Branden said, calmer by a fraction. "Let's try to keep it at one homicide a day."

"What have you got, Mike?" Robertson said. "Give."

"I think there's an Amish kid buried in a barn back up a little drive off of 58."

"You think?" Bruce asked.

"There's a body out here, Bruce. Cal is watching the place so nobody disturbs the scene any more."

"Any more than what?" Robertson asked.

"We kind of tracked the place up with an Amish girl just now, before we found the body," Branden said. "We didn't know there was a body until we started digging. There was some stuff belonging to a John Schlabaugh in a plastic bag buried on top of the body."

"I'm gonna want you to voucher all of that when I get out there. I'll want to talk to that girl, too."

"OK, Bruce, but our Amish girl has fled already."

"Dang, Mike!"

"We didn't know it was a crime scene until later, when we found the body. Then, she bolted. Took off in a red Firebird belonging to John Schlabaugh. Couldn't stop her. Left her horse and buggy behind."

"OK, look," Robertson said, "just don't disturb anything until I get Missy out there."

"I'll have to show you where it is."

"So meet us somewhere."

"OK, meet me at the intersection where 129 comes down off the ridge and tees into 58. The barn's not far from there."

Robertson said, "Give us ten minutes," and switched off.

*   *   *

Branden tried the number for Abe Yoder's cell phone again. This time the phone was not in service. He turned his truck around, waited for a pair of Amish women on bicycles to clear the intersection, and drove halfway back down 129. At the end of the long drive up to the Wallace place, he spotted Sergeant Ricky Niell on the right berm.

Niell got in with the professor and waved for one of the sheriff's cruisers to follow. A second cruiser stayed parked at the end of the Wallace drive, blocking the way in.

Branden pushed hard down the long stretch of 129 to the T-intersection with 58 and pulled off to the right, under a stand of hickory trees, to wait for Robertson. The cruiser with two of Niell's deputies pulled off the road behind him.

"You ever heard of a murdered Amish kid?" Niell asked.

"No," Branden said. He pounded the steering wheel and groaned, "I let her get away. Sara Yoder."

Ricky pointed down the road and said, "Here they come."

Branden pulled out onto 58 ahead of Robertson's cruiser, and led two squad cars, with lights flashing and sirens blaring, to the red barn where Cal waited.

Inside the sliding doors, Robertson studied the shallow grave and then the dirt on the floor of the barn and said, "You really tracked it up good, Mike."

The coroner, Melissa Taggert, maneuvered the big sheriff off to the side and said, "This is my crime scene, now, boys, so give me some room to work."

Robertson lumbered back outside, gathered Branden, Troyer, and Niell together, and said, "Missy's going to go over things in there, and then she's going to want to take the body in to the morgue." To Niell he said, "Ricky, get Dan Wilsher on the radio and have him bring out Missy's wagon."

To Branden, Robertson said, "I need that girl's name, Professor."

Branden said, "Sara Yoder. Cal can tell you where she lives."

Robertson turned to Cal, who said, "It's one of several houses in a compound over on Mechanic Township 110. You go out through Saltillo and take the first right. That puts you on 68. Then another right puts you on T-110. She lives down in a little valley opposite the old Salem Cemetery. It's a large collection of houses, relatives living close together. If you're sending someone over there, I should go along, make sure we get the right house."

When Ricky Niell came back from making his radio call, Robertson said, "Ricky, I want you to take Cal out there and see if you can find this girl. Take Armbruster's cruiser, there."

Niell nodded, said, "Right. What kind of car was she driving?"

Branden said, "A red '77 or '78 Pontiac Firebird. Has that long hood. And aluminum racing wheels."

"It ought to stick out like a sore thumb around here," Ricky said.

As Niell and Cal got into the cruiser, Robertson said, "Find her fast, Ricky. If she bolted like that, she knows something. Or she's running scared because she did this. Or knows who did."

Niell leaned out the window and said, "I've still got men at the Wallace place."

"You saw the blood in his kitchen?" Robertson asked.

Niell nodded.

"I want them looking for Wallace. Blood in his kitchen and a murdered kid here, so close, it can't be a coincidence."

"Good luck," Branden said. "If Spits Wallace is dug in back there in the woods, it'll take a commando team to force him out."

4

WHILE Coroner Taggert uncovered the body inside the barn with the help of Ricky Niell's two deputies, Robertson paced in the heat of the barn's doorway, dabbed at the back of his neck with a red checkered bandanna, and listened to Branden. Branden gave the sheriff an account of his conversation with Sara Yoder that morning.

Branden finished with, "I suppose you'll consider her a witness to something, Bruce, but I can't believe she'd bring us out here if she had anything to do with murder."

"It's not just Sara Yoder," Robertson said. He folded the bandanna and pushed it into his hip pocket. "By her account, there are seven to nine Amish kids running together, and one of them is apparently dead."

"We don't know who the dead one is at this point. It wouldn't necessarily have to be anyone of her group."

"Yeah, but she has a pretty good idea who it is, taking off the way she did."

"Bruce, she'd have fled no matter who was in that grave. Just seeing a body would be enough to send her off, and if she has an idea who it is, then that's immeasurably worse."

"Why didn't you just keep her here, Mike?"

"How? Tell me that. What was I supposed to do, run her off the road with my truck? Look, Cal knows where she lives, and she

26

has a cell phone. One way or another, she's going to turn up. But, she brought us out here, and that means she's not involved in a murder."

"I wouldn't expect an Amish girl to be mixed up in murder, Mike, under any circumstances. But Amish kids out on the Rumschpringe get into trouble all the time. You know they do. All kinds of stupid trouble."

Missy Taggert walked over from the grave and said, "Trouble, yes. But they don't as a rule get themselves shot, Bruce."

Robertson and the professor stepped toward the grave, and Missy warded them off with an outstretched palm. "I'm not done."

"Shot how?" Robertson asked.

"Shot in the side of the head, with a large-caliber pistol, and at short range," Missy said. "First I've ever heard of an Amish kid who got murdered."

"How long's he been dead?" Robertson asked.

"Several days," Missy said. "Maybe a week. I'll be able to tell you more once I get him up to the lab."

Branden asked, "Did you find any identification on the body, Missy? Driver's license or credit cards?"

"Nothing."

"Who do you think it is?" Robertson asked the professor.

"John Schlabaugh. Abe Yoder, maybe."

"That's whose cell phone you found?" Robertson asked.

"It was Abe Yoder's phone, but it was in a bag with John Schlabaugh's things."

"Who is that?" Missy asked.

Branden frowned. "John Schlabaugh is the leader of a little band of Amish kids who've taken the Rumschpringe much too far."

Missy studied the professor a moment, shook her head sadly, and said, "I'm going to finish up in here, now, so how's about you two giving us some room to work? I'll want to load the body and get a series of pictures all around. I'd like the state crime lab to go over the barn for trace evidence. That OK?"

Robertson said, "Sure, Missy. We'll clear out. Call in who you need," and he grimly led Branden out into the sun.

In front of the barn, Deputy Stan Armbruster and Captain Dan Wilsher were waiting with the coroner's station wagon. Wilsher lifted his chin toward the barn and said, "Dead Amish kid in there?"

"Yeah," Robertson said. "Missy has the body about ready to go. Gunshot wound to the side of the head."

Wilsher whistled. "Never thought I'd see the day."

Robertson said, "We're looking for Sara Yoder, Dan. She ran with a group. John Schlabaugh was the leader, it seems, and that might be him in the barn. There is also evidently an Abe Yoder involved."

Wilsher wrote the names in a spiral notebook, and said, "If that's John Schlabaugh, then I think we'd better bring the Drug Enforcement Administration in on this."

"DEA?" Branden said, surprised.

Robertson said, "They've had a quiet investigation going on in the Saltillo area for the last ten months. Saltillo, Charm, and thereabouts, anyway. It's more than just a little marijuana from time to time. Kids have been scoring Ecstasy from a dealer down in Columbus. Dan's been my liaison with the DEA for several months now."

Wilsher added, "John Schlabaugh's name has appeared in reports I've read on drug activity here. The DEA is holding off on arrests until they can get the top people in the outfit that's wholesaling the drugs. But John Schlabaugh will be a priority with them when they do finally decide to make some arrests. If he isn't already dead."

Branden nodded unhappily and said, "Then you should know that Sara Yoder intimated to Cal and me that some calamity was going to occur because of something Abe Yoder and John Schlabaugh had done down there in Columbus. I suspect she was talking about drugs."

"The DEA team will know about it, if Amish're involved with the Columbus outfit," Wilsher said. "They've got a man undercover down there."

Robertson said, "OK, then. We've got to bring Sara Yoder in. And I mean fast. I also want to talk to other members of this Schlabaugh crew."

"I don't have any other names," Branden said.

"Cal's gonna know that," Robertson asserted, and pointed down the lane.

Ricky Niell's cruiser pulled up fast behind the coroner's station wagon, and Niell and Cal Troyer got out. Niell reported, "We found the red Pontiac in a culvert. Beside the Salem Cemetery. No sign of the girl. I called in Johnson to guard it. We'll need a team to go through it for evidence."

Branden asked, "What about the cell phone she took?"

Cal held it up and said, "It was still plugged into the cigarette lighter."

Robertson took the phone and handed it to Captain Wilsher. "Dan," he said. "See what this cell can tell us."

Wilsher said, "Right. You want the car towed?"

Robertson nodded. Wilsher got into Ricky Niell's cruiser and started making radio calls.

Robertson said, "Ricky, you see what you can do to help inside," and turned to Cal Troyer. "Cal, I need to find this Sara Yoder."

Cal said, "I don't know where she's gone, Bruce. Her parents don't know either. We checked at her house. The bishop was there, visiting."

In the distance, a buggy could be heard rattling briskly up the lane. Robertson, Troyer, and Branden walked to meet it, the sheriff and the professor instinctively letting Cal take the lead. Cal stepped up on the driver's side of the black buggy and spoke a few lines of old Dutch dialect to an elderly Amish gentleman with a weathered face and long white chin whiskers, tinted yellow at the corners of his mouth. His denim suit was old and worn, and his vest was un-hooked in front. He took off his battered straw hat, wiped out the sweatband with a wrinkled handkerchief, and put the hat back carefully on his head. To Troyer he said, "We understand there's a body in the barn."

Robertson stepped forward and said, "It's a younger fellow dressed in Amish clothes." He waited a beat, stuck out his hand, and added, "I'm Sheriff Bruce Robertson."

"I know that," the man said and took Robertson's hand lightly. "Bishop Irvin Raber. I voted for you in '92."

"I appreciate the confidence," Robertson said.

"Didn't say I voted for you any time since," Raber said.

Robertson let that pass and said, "Bishop Raber, it'll help us if you could take a look at the body. Tell us who it is."

Raber stroked his chin whiskers, looked at Cal Troyer, and said to Robertson, "It's not the kind of thing you think you'll ever have to do when you're called to serve as bishop. Identify a murdered soul."

Raber got down gingerly from the seat of the buggy. Robertson led him into the barn, and Troyer and Branden waited by the buggy. The bishop soon came out alone, looking somber, and climbed up to the springy wooden seat of his rig. He shook his head, took off his wire-rimmed glasses, and pinched the bridge of his nose. "You never know how far you can let the kids go, Cal," he said, an ago-nizing sorrow in his eyes.

"They have to find their own way, Irvin," Cal said softly. "They have to come to the faith of their own choosing."

Raber brought his gaze to meet Cal's, studied the pastor's ex-pression, and sighed heavily. "Now I have to go tell his parents."

He slapped the reins, and Cal and Branden stepped back from the buggy. Raber swung out in a wide circle, said, "I'll send some-one out here for Sara Yoder's buggy," and headed his clattering rig back down the lane.

Robertson came out of the barn as the deputies were wrestling a loaded body bag into the back of Missy Taggert's station wagon.

The sheriff walked over to Troyer and Branden slowly, rubbing the bristles of his gray crew cut with his red bandanna.

"Bishop says it's John Schlabaugh who's been murdered," he said.

Branden watched the buggy disappear behind the trees that lined the lane and said, "John Schlabaugh dead, and Abe and Sara Yoder missing. That leaves six to talk to, and who knows where any of them will be."

Robertson said, "I just hope they're all alive."

"What in the world is going on, Bruce?" Branden asked.

"It's been getting worse every year," Robertson said. "Sooner or later it was going to end up being really big trouble. Now we've got it in spades."

Branden turned to face the pond behind the barn. His eyes fell on the treeline at the far edge of the cornfield. He turned in place and studied the quiet green of the forest that bordered the lane, then the far edge of the tall corn, and last the red barn. "Who owns this property?" he asked the sheriff.

"Beats me."

"Why would an Amish kid keep a Pontiac Firebird in somebody's barn?"

Robertson grunted, shrugged.

"What are Amish kids doing with cell phones and GPS trackers?"

"The cell phones I get," Robertson said.

"Amish never used to use phones," Branden said.

"It's the wire," Cal said, "not the phone."

Robertson said, "What?"

"It was always the wire that Amish folk objected to. If you hook your house up to a wire from a public utility or other concern, then you're not living the life of a completely autonomous peasant farmer. You've lost your independence. You've become ever more attached to the world outside the church. Amish resist that in every form."

"Phones were OK, but the wires weren't?" Robertson asked.

"Something like that," Cal said. "There aren't many English who understand this point, but cell phones don't have wires. So the bishop never has to ask why you've got that phone. No wire, no phone. At least there's no need for the bishop to make an example out of anyone."

"That's the screwiest dang thing I ever heard of," Robertson said.

"You may think so, but there are more cell phones tucked under pillows out here than you'd ever believe."

Branden said, "Then it's not too much of a rebellion for John Schlabaugh's Amish gang to have used cell phones."

Cal said, "No, it's not. The GPS receivers, though, that's a little bit different. That's satellite technology. Cell phones are just fancy radios. I don't know any bishops who have had to rule on the things, but it might come to that. Somebody's going to bring it up, and then the bishops will have to come to some decisions about GPS receivers. The objectionable technology comes from satellites in space. They'll consider that worse than phones."

"Cell phones, and those GPS receivers," Robertson said. "What else do we know about the Schlabaugh gang?"

"They've been having parties," Branden said.

"And making trips to Columbus," Cal said.

"Drugs again," Robertson said.

"Wouldn't be the first time," Branden said.

Dan Wilsher came over with Abe Yoder's cell phone. "There's quite a list of numbers in the address book," he said. "And there's a key code of integers, 1, 2, 3, like that, that are assigned to each of nine names. Amish names as far as I can tell."

Robertson asked, "How about a log of incoming and outgoing calls?"

"That, too," Wilsher said.

"OK, Dan. You run with the phone. Get phone company records, everything. I want to know who's been calling whom, and when. I want to know where they were standing when they made those calls. I want to know it yesterday."

Robertson called Niell over and said, "We still have the Spits Wallace thing. Any ideas?"

"Nobody's been in that kitchen for a while," Ricky said. "The food in the sink is all shriveled up, and the blood is dried. You can see that just standing at a window."

Robertson said, "Dan, I'll meet you back at the jail in an hour. In the meantime, Doc Branden and I are going to go over to the Wallace place to have a look around."

Niell said, "The coroner wants more pictures, so I'll hang back."

Robertson countered, "Negative, Ricky. I want you and Cal back out looking for Sara Yoder."

Niell said, a little surprised, "No problem."

"Anything else you want us to work on?" Wilsher asked, squinting in the sun.

Robertson thought, looked around, and said, "Try to find out who owns this barn. But, Dan, Sara Yoder is the thing we've got to work on first. If Ricky needs more men, send them out. Call in men on overtime if you have to. We've got to find her, and she's been gone a good hour now. Everybody rolls on this one, Dan. I want everybody we've got out looking for that girl. I want her found, and I mean right now."

5

Friday, July 23
10:50 A.M.

IT WAS a tight fit for Bruce Robertson in the passenger seat of the professor's small white truck, and when they pulled up to the Wallace place on high ground north of 129, the sheriff popped himself out before the engine was silent. Branden got out and scanned the property, while Robertson stood beside the truck, stretching his legs and taking deeper breaths as he studied the Wallace abode. The cruiser that had been parked at the end of the long drive pulled in behind Branden's truck.

Spits Wallace occupied a ramshackle, two-story, plain white clapboard house with a big porch that pitched forward from the front of the house under the weight of a dozen rusted appliances, everything from cast-off washers and dryers to a refrigerator with its door off the hinges. The dirty white siding of the house had apparently last been painted when Spits Wallace had been a young boy. The untended roof shingles hung out over the gutters, taking a slow slide into dilapidation.

Behind the house was a crude carport with a cracked, corrugated, green plastic roof covered with wet leaves and supported by unconfident poles, the whole thing taking a lean out of plumb as if the weight of years was more than it could bear.

To the left of the stone drive, set off about fifty paces and almost hidden by dense, new-growth forest, squatted the remains of a log cabin so old it might reasonably have been considered colonial. The jumbled pile of weathered logs had caved in over its center, the victim of a slow and tortured implosion into ruin.

Branden switched off his cell phone and went around the front of the truck to stand next to Robertson. The sheriff asked, "You know how to get into this house without getting our heads blown off?"

Branden chuckled. "Unless Spits Wallace has learned a thing or two about booby traps since his father owned the place."

"Great," Robertson breathed. "Just great."

"In through the back kitchen door is best," Branden said and led the sheriff around a disordered pile of old furniture and battered crates to a door at the back of the house.

Robertson peered through a high window over a sink, and Branden tried the screened door.

"It's still open," Branden said, and let the door swing back shut.

"Can't see anything through the window," Robertson said. He walked over, opened the screened door, and stuck his head into the kitchen.

From behind, they heard the metallic snap and click of a shotgun action, and when they turned around, a dirty and ill-clad Spits Wallace was standing twenty feet behind them with a double-barreled shotgun draped across the crook of his left arm. With his right hand, he had a nervous grip on the stock and trigger.

"Spits," Robertson said.

"Sheriff."

Robertson heard his deputies climbing out of the cruiser behind him, and he turned and waved them back into their seats.

Wallace said, "You've got me outnumbered, Sheriff. Send your men away."

"Now, why would I do that, Spits?"

"I'll plug you good, if you don't all get off my property."

Robertson turned to his deputies and made a hand signal. The cruiser backed slowly down the drive. Then Robertson turned back to Wallace.

Spits Wallace was a short man with an erratic beard. Bald at the top, he had a nose like a hawk and rheumy eyes. His fingers were bent with arthritis, and his grip on the shotgun kept slipping. He had an involuntary twitch under his left eye, and his face screwed up into a painful grimace each time he shifted his weight on his bowed legs. Brown clay and gray mud caked his clothes, face, and boots, and his forehead was streaked as black as soot. Behind him was parked an old rusty wheelbarrow stacked full of irregular lumps of coal.

"You in the habit of greeting company with iron, there, Spits?" Robertson asked coolly.

"When it suits me," Wallace said evenly, and spat tobacco at his feet.

"How about you show us some hospitality, Spits," Robertson barked. "Explain that blood my boys found in your kitchen."

Wallace spat again and wiped a brown dribble from his bearded chin with the back of his hand. He studied both men intently and grunted disapproval. "How's about you boys just clear on out of here and leave me be."

"When you explain about the blood," Robertson said.

"Cut myself shaving. So, I reckon you boys oughta leave."

"I used to know your father," Branden said. "Back when I was a kid. I'd come out with my dad when he'd to try to sell your dad insurance on his gold coins. You and I played one day over in your cave while they talked."

Wallace leveled his gaze at Branden, a mixture of disdain and alarm in his eyes. "My dad never needed any insurance dandies to tell him how to take care of his gold."

Robertson said, "Maybe your gold has something to do with the bloodstains on your kitchen wall."

"You got it wrong, Sheriff. It was my dad who had the gold. I got nothing."

"Your neighbors told us they heard shots over here a while back, and they haven't seen you in a spell," Robertson said.

"My neighbors don't know how to mind their own business," Spits said and spat again, this time closer to Robertson.

Robertson stared back at Wallace for a dozen beats of his heart, nodded at the wheelbarrow behind the man, and said, "You've been over to the old strip mines."

"What if I have?"

"Nothing. It might account for why you need a bath, is all."

Wallace eyed the sheriff, laughed scornfully, and spat again.

Branden said, "A young Amish boy's been murdered, Spits. Over east of 58. It's not that far from here. You know anything about that?"

Wallace stared back at the professor wordlessly.

Branden asked, "You ever see any Amish kids out in these parts?"

"We got Amish all over the place. You know that, Branden, good as anybody does."

"Do you know John Schlabaugh from Saltillo?" Branden asked.

"Might."

"He's been shot."

Wallace's brow knitted almost imperceptibly and his eyes flashed brief heat. "Then I reckon he mixed in with the wrong crowd."

"What do you know about it?" Robertson tried.

"I know his little gang of kids. Every one of them. They use those old summer cabins for parties. I've run 'em off my property a couple of times."

"When was the last time you saw any of them?" Robertson asked.

Wallace chewed and spat, and scratched at a scab on his wrist. He thought about an answer and hesitated.

Branden said, "John Schlabaugh's been shot, Spits. He's dead. If you can tell us something that'd be helpful, I'd be grateful."

"For old times' sake?" Wallace scowled.

"Like I said. I knew your dad. He used to take me and my father through your house. Showed us his collection of coins, in all those old canvas bags. Stuffed under all the furniture. Stacked in the closets."

"Ain't got no gold," Wallace spat. "I'm tired of telling people that."

Robertson said, "We're not here because of your gold."

"I don't have no gold!" Wallace shouted.

Robertson took a step forward, and Wallace shouldered the shotgun and barked, "You boys stand where you're at!"

Robertson froze, stared at the 12-gauge barrels, and tried to relax. "Easy, there, Spits," he said. "Just tell us what you know about John Schlabaugh."

Wallace croaked out an angry growl, stepped forward, pointed his shotgun at Branden's truck, and said, "You boys get back in your truck and don't do anything I don't tell you to do."

Branden eased back several paces, and Robertson matched him. Slowly the two men moved back to the truck. When they were seated with the doors closed, Wallace said, shotgun still at the ready, "Now buckle up, gents."

Both men did that.

"Now start her up, Branden, and back it up around here so's you're pointed back the way you came."

Branden did that.

Wallace stalked up to Robertson on the passenger side and said his piece, punctuating the space in front of the sheriff's nose with the muzzle of his shotgun.

"Last I saw of John Schlabaugh, that dirty little brat and his pal Abe Yoder were leading a gang of three city slickers up to my back door. But I don't like visitors, see, so I made myself scarce.

"It's like I keep telling everybody. I AIN'T GOT NO GOLD!"

6

WHEN Ricky Niell and Cal Troyer made it back to the valley along
Township Lane T-110 where Sara Yoder had left the Pontiac in the
ditch beside the Salem Cemetery, the Firebird was being hooked up
for a tow. From where they stood on the east ridge, they could see
the several houses and barns of the Yoder compound on the other
side of the wide valley. Through the heat shimmers across the long,
hazy distance, they could see the trunk and rear bumper of an old
black car in the doorway of a barn. They turned Niell's cruiser
around, drove back down County 68 to the creek, crossed to the
other side of the valley under tall shade trees, and took the long
gravel drive back to the Yoder houses. When they parked the cruiser
and got out behind what proved to be a '50s model black Ford Fair-
lane with no license plate, there were several Amish children, a mix
of ages, milling around the old car. One little fellow had planted
himself behind the steering wheel, turning it left and right, bounc-
ing on his seat, and making a grrr sound like an engine. When the
other kids saw Niell's black and gray uniform, they backed shyly
away from the car. Eventually, the boy behind the wheel noticed the
new tension in his brothers and sisters, turned and saw Niell and
Troyer, and climbed sheepishly out of the car. All the kids backed
up a pace, but none of them took the opportunity to leave.

An Amish woman in a light green dress, white apron, and white
head covering with loose tie strings came out the side door of the

adjoining house. She walked across the grass in plain black shoes and black stockings, carrying a wadded handkerchief. Her eyes were red and her lids were puffy.

To Ricky, she said, "Can I help you?" and held the handkerchief to her eyes.

"Ma'am, I'm Sergeant Niell, and this is Cal Troyer."

"I know the pastor, Sergeant," she said and acknowledged Troyer with a respectful nod.

"Ma'am, we're looking for Sara Yoder," Niell said.

"She's my niece, Sergeant. Is she in trouble, too?"

"The sheriff wants to talk with her. It's very important. Urgent, you might say."

"You'll need to talk with my husband," she said cautiously.

"I'd also like to talk with the children," Niell said and took out a pocket notebook and one of his gold pens. "And I'd like to write down some names, so I know more about your family."

Sara's aunt hesitated and looked to Cal for reassurance.

Cal said, "We don't think she's in any trouble with the law. She may be in some danger, though, so you should know that, Miriam. We'd like to ask her some questions about John Schlabaugh. The way we understand it, she parked that Pontiac over by the cemetery."

Miriam Yoder stiffened and glanced nervously at the children standing nearby. In dialect, she spoke several words, and the younger children scurried away toward the house. Three older boys took up positions behind her.

"My husband's name is Albert Yoder. That's Albert P. Yoder. He's got a cousin Albert O. Yoder. I am Miriam Yoder. These boys here saw Sara leave the car over by the cemetery."

Mrs. Yoder turned and spoke Dutch at some length to one of the three boys. He gave a long answer, also in dialect. Turning back to Niell and Troyer, she answered, simply, "She left in a car with two English."

Cal gave Ricky a look of alarm, moved off twenty feet, and made a hushed call on his cell phone.

Niell studied the faces of the three lads behind Mrs. Yoder and concluded that they had been less than forthright. Or perhaps that Mrs. Yoder had not provided a complete translation of everything the lad had said.

An Amish gentleman joined the group from around the corner of the barn. He was soon joined by two other men who came down the gravel lane from the direction of the other houses. Miriam Yoder backed up a yard or so to allow the men to come forward on the gravel pad in front of the barn.

The first man, an older gentleman with a bushy gray beard and thinning gray hair, said, "I am Albert Yoder, Officer." His eyes, too, were red.

Cal returned to Niell's side, and Albert Yoder greeted him, "Pastor."

"Albert," replied Cal, and put his cell phone away.

"I'm at a little disadvantage, Mr. Yoder," Niell said. "You all seem to know Pastor Troyer, here."

Mr. Yoder nodded gravely and said, "We've not been hospitable, Sergeant." He turned and spoke soft Dutch to Miriam, and she went back to the house.

Albert said, "Please join us on the porch. I'll make introductions."

Niell glanced at Cal for guidance, and Cal nodded agreement, following Yoder toward the house.

In the yard between the barn and the two-story house, a volleyball net was stretched above a level patch of grass. A concrete path lined with petunias and edged with red bricks passed behind the volleyball court and circumnavigated a large round trampoline with thick plastic padding around its edges. A wooden swing set and two tall wooden poles holding white purple martin houses stood against the azure sky. The children followed the men in a tight group, staying down at lawn level when the men went up the steps of the porch.

On the porch, there were three long deacon's benches, and the Amish men took seats on one of them. Albert Yoder indicated large,

41

deep wicker chairs for Niell and Troyer. When they were all seated, Ricky and Cal found themselves looking slightly up at the stern Amish men.

Miriam Yoder came out the screened door with a tray of paper cups and a pitcher of lemonade. She set the tray on a round, glass-topped table in front of Albert Yoder's knees and then poured five cups of lemonade before going back into the house.

Albert Yoder handed lemonade to each of the men, Troyer and Niell first. The Amish men sipped quietly at their drinks. Cal took one sip to be polite and held the cup in his lap. Niell drank it all down straight and put the empty cup back on the tray, agonizing over the crawling pace of the conversation.

"Thanks," Niell said. "And thank your wife, would you?"

Yoder said, "Now, Sergeant Niell, introductions. As I said, I am Albert P. Yoder. Here is also Willis Stutzman and one of my cousins, Albert O. Yoder. Albert O. is father to Sara Yoder, and I am father to Abe Yoder. Abe and Sara run with the Schlabaugh gang. Willis Stutzman is father to one of the boys who also runs with John Schlabaugh. He is a close neighbor."

Niell thanked Yoder for the introductions and said, "I presume you all know about John Schlabaugh?"

Albert said, "The bishop was just here. We need to be getting over to the Schlabaughs' house pretty soon. They are all tucked in at home, waiting for us to help."

"I won't keep you long," Niell said, taking a small notebook out of his breast pocket.

Cal touched Niell's arm, eyeing the notebook. Niell shrugged and put the notebook back into his uniform shirt pocket, trusting that Cal Troyer would know best how to proceed.

Niell said, "I need your help. If you know where Sara Yoder is, I need you to tell us."

Albert P. Yoder said, "I'll tell you what we know, Sergeant. Sara Yoder drove off with some men about an hour ago. She left John Schlabaugh's car out on the road, and a deputy came by later to have it towed. It is good riddance as far as I am concerned. Now we do not know where Sara went, and we haven't seen anything of Abe, my son, for over a month."

"Are you not speaking with your son, Mr. Yoder?" Niell asked.

Yoder turned pensive and tangled his fingers in his chin whiskers. To the boys on the lawn he said, "You youngsters run along, now. You have chores."

The boys left, obviously disappointed.

Yoder gave a quick glance to the men sitting with him on the bench and evidently saw enough encouragement in their expressions that he decided to talk. "Abe quit on my 14/7," he said. "I reckon he knows not to come back until he's made a few changes."

"14/7?" asked Niell.

"It's the financial arrangement I use to let him stay with us even though he's of an age to marry."

Cal asked, "Albert, do you know what kind of thing Abe and John had gotten mixed up in while they've been running together?"

"The usual running around wild, I suppose," Yoder said.

Willis Stutzman coughed pointedly, and Albert said, "OK, well, maybe more than the usual wild behavior. Willis can tell you better."

Willis Stutzman appeared to Niell to be about ten years younger than Albert P. Yoder. He was dressed in blue denim trousers and a pink short-sleeved shirt under black braces. He eased forward on the deacon's bench and leaned over, elbows on knees, to light his pipe. When he had it going he said, "My oldest boy, Andy, wants to marry Sara Yoder, but she's not of a mind."

He glanced sideways through the smoke at Albert O. Yoder, Sara's father, and the man shrugged apologetically, as if Stutzman had spoken a well-known fact.

Stutzman continued. "It often develops that a man, gone courting, has to wait for the girl to make up her mind. But, when this Rumschpringe started up, quite a few of the kids took it too far. We Amish allow the Rumschpringe so that the children can learn what the English world is really like. So they can see what they are turning away from, if they choose to be Amish like us. That's the only way they can be certain of their choice. If they didn't burn it out of their systems, they would wonder all their lives what they had missed in the world. So, Amish allow the Rumschpringe, and have allowed it for many generations. But that doesn't mean we approve of wild behavior. The children live with us, work with us, eat with us, and then sometimes, usually on a weekend, they just go away for a spell. Change their clothes to English and then go to town. We don't follow them around, so we're not ever really sure where they go, or what they do.

"We allow this because it is all necessary for a true, informed, adult decision to join the church. It's the best way for them and us to know that they are taking their vows seriously."

That said, Stutzman sat up straight and drew several puffs on his pipe, as if he thought he had said everything a soul could ever want to know on the matter.

Sara's father, Albert O. Yoder, said, "If she comes back, everything will be forgiven. Tell her that, Sergeant Niell."

Niell tapped a thumb on his knee and considered what had been said. He shifted to a more upright posture and said, "Are you telling me you don't even know where Sara might be?"

"Yes," answered her father.

"Or that you can't tell us where she typically goes on the weekends?"

An affirmative nod of Yoder's head.

"Who she hangs with in the English world?"

Unhappy shrugs from all three of the men.

Albert P. Yoder cleared his throat and stood up. Bishop Irvin Raber climbed the steps to the porch, and the men stood up briefly and then sat down when the bishop sat. Albert P. Yoder introduced Niell to the bishop, and Niell stood to shake his hand.

When both men were seated again, the bishop said, "We'll hold the services for John Schlabaugh as soon as we can. The Schlabaughs are on hard times, as you know, from their daughter's medi-

cal bills, so they're going to need help with the food for the day."
When he had handed each Amish man a slip of paper with figures
written out for their family's contributions, he finished by asking
Niell, "Will we be able to have the body soon, Sergeant?"

"I can't say, Mr. Raber," Niell said. "The coroner will make that
decision."

Willis Stutzman and Albert O. bent to each other's ears and whispered in dialect.

The bishop said, "We shouldn't be rude." To Niell he explained,
"The men were commenting that the coroner is a woman."

Niell nodded, and said enthusiastically, "She is. She's Sheriff
Robertson's wife. And she's the best coroner in any county around
here. The body will be released just as soon as she says it's OK."

"Then we may have to go forward with the memorial services
without a body," the bishop replied. "We need to do this so that
the Schlabaughs can come to grips with John's death. To give them
some closure. A period to grieve."

Niell nodded and pursed his lips. "I'll find out what I can and
let you know. What's the best way to reach you?"

Bishop Irvin Raber cast an amused glance at each of the three
Amish men. He said, "Each of these men has a cell phone. I suppose it'd do to call one of them, if they'll be forthcoming enough
to give you their numbers."

While Ricky Niell wrote down phone numbers for the cell
phones, Bishop Raber drew Cal aside on the lawn in front of the
porch and offered to drive the pastor back into town in his buggy.
Understanding the meaning of the bishop's offer, Cal accepted and
suggested that Niell go back to town ahead of him.

As Ricky was getting behind the wheel of his cruiser out on the
lane, Cal ducked down and whispered urgently, "Ricky, you didn't
get the whole truth back there. It's typical Amish caution, wanting
to avoid entanglement with the law. But, Sara Yoder didn't just get
in a car with two English men the way Miriam said. That's not what
the boy told her. The boy told her that the two English men pulled

Sara out of that Firebird and forced her into their car. A big white SUV."

"She's been kidnapped?" Ricky said incredulously.

"That's the phone call I made while you were talking to Miriam. To tell Robertson that she has been abducted."

Ricky shook his head, angry at the backwardness that had caused the bishop to withhold crucial information. "When are they ever going to trust us, Cal?"

"I'm gonna work on that right now," Cal said. "Try to coax Raber into a better posture toward law enforcement. But I can't predict how he'll respond. I know these people out here. They're not at all big on government authority."

Ricky tapped the steering wheel with both of this thumbs. "How long's it been, Cal? An hour and a half since you saw her?"

"About that."

Ricky shook his head again.

Cal said, "It's slow with the Amish, Ricky."

"Do they all understand, you think, that she was abducted?"

"I'm sure they do."

"Then what's the problem?"

"They don't easily trust English, and they don't trust law enforcement at all, Ricky. They have long memories of their martyr history in Europe before their ancestors came to America."

"I'm still going to knock on some doors out here, Cal. See what I can learn."

"OK, Ricky. I'll have Raber drop me off at the jailhouse when we get back to town. But, take it slow with these people. You've got two strikes against you just by wearing your uniform."

7

Friday, July 23
11:30 A.M.

SLOWLY, Troyer and Raber paced down the gravel lane to its intersection with County Road 68, near the little iron bridge where
the creek crossed the valley. There the bishop had his house and a
small furniture shop. His buggy was a simple open hack, and it
took little more than a minute to harness a chestnut Standardbred
to the rig. Riding high on the buckboard, the two men headed back
toward Salem Cemetery on Mechanic Township Lane T-110, the
bishop letting the horse set an ambling pace.

As they rode, Bishop Raber and Cal talked about the twenty-
three families in the bishop's small church, many of whom Cal knew
well. The mothers and fathers and grandparents. Courtships, children, troubles with health, genetic concerns, and infractions of a
slight and a sometimes serious nature. Raber told how the church
had been supporting one family whose father had lost an arm in a
sawmill accident. How the man was expected to find suitable work
once he had mended. How the older boys would have to take up
the slack until that happened.

He told of the precocious young girl with the withered leg who
probably never would be able to marry, not so much because of her
physical infirmity, but because of her fatalistic outlook on life. He
spoke of the prevalence of certain hereditary traits in the small
community. There were three dwarfs in the church. There were

also exotic genetic disorders that researchers from Ohio State University wanted his permission to study. And Raber spoke poignantly of the heartache several families were enduring, a heartache made infinitely worse by the day's events, as their children stretched their Rumschpringes to lengths that were not believed to be reversible.

He came eventually to the subject of John Schlabaugh, not because of John's open rebellion, but, surprisingly, because of the abundant crops John was able to bring in for the farmers in the church, using the tractor he had bought after selling his land.

Cal asked about that, and Raber explained. Young Schlabaugh had inherited a patch of arable land in the prosperous Doughty Valley, to the south of the high ground at Saltillo. He kept the barn and a single-wide trailer on two acres and sold the rest of the land for a handsome price. And that, Raber explained, was the problem. The very root of it, as far as he was concerned. A young man with nothing to do and too much money on his hands.

Cal listened and gradually came to appreciate the true nature of the dilemma the bishop faced. Before today, John Schlabaugh's fate could have swung one way or another, and it would have signified nothing more than the good or bad standing in the church of a single boy. They had lost others to the world before, and knew that heartache well. They had learned how to go on. But if Raber, as bishop, were ever to have ruled against Schlabaugh's tractor, the men of the whole church would have lost the advantage at harvest that the tractor, hired out to each family in rotation, had provided. That would have put a stop to the extra cash crops the men were able to plant each year. And without the money from those crops, the families who needed cash in emergency rooms could not be helped. The doctor bills for a girl with a withered leg could not be paid. The families would not have the ready cash the bishop would need for the farmer whose barn burned down after a lightning strike. Or for funerals. The social fabric of his district would start to unravel at the economic seams. To rule against the tractor had never been practical.

Still, young Schlabaugh had proved himself a ne'er-do-well, and the allure of his rebellious fife had piped too many children into rebellion. All this Cal surmised, and more.

At a pause, Cal asked, "Maybe the tractor could be sold to a co-operative English family?"

Bishop Raber tightened the reins and brought the buggy to a halt at the intersection of T-110 and County 19, just west of Becks Mills. Here was the center of the long Doughty Valley, where the barns were, for the most part, tall and new. Bright red in the summer sun. Fields planted luxuriantly in all directions. A lazy, sandy stream cutting a meandering channel through the fields. A lone hawk, circling in the blue overhead. Cars as rare here as buggies were in town.

Beside the bishop's buggy, a white board fence framed a pasture where three Belgian draft horses nibbled the grass, tails swishing. A lad on a flatbed wagon, pulled by a Halflinger, turned into the lane with sacks of dogfood and grass seed stacked behind him on the rough boards. Two Amish kids rode by on expensive bicycles, new and shiny. Bishop Raber took in the surrounding countryside and said, "My district stops here, Cal, at County 19. John Schlabaugh's place is up the way, left a quarter mile, on the left side of the road. At least that's where he's been living since he left home.

"The Schlabaughs are good people. There are six boys and four girls so far, and every one of them toes the line. Everyone except John."

With that, the bishop fell silent and started the horse again. Taking 19 west, he came to the intersection where County 58 dumped out into the Doughty Valley, west of Panther Hollow. The bishop stopped the buggy again, on the flat bridge over Mullet Run. He looked up at the blue sky overhead, and then let his eyes drift down to the stream coursing under the bridge.

Cal asked, "Who will get John's property, now that he's gone?"

Raber answered, "Who would expect an eighteen-year-old boy to have written out a will?"

"Would his father try to keep the tractor?"

Raber shook his head and said, "I have decided to rule out tractors. Whatever the hardship, we have got to go back to the land. To tend the land as our fathers did. No, tractors are out. When harvest comes, we'll help each other bring in what crops we can, and then the English can take the rest for a price. Next year, we'll plant only what we need."

"John Schlabaugh blazed quite a trail through your district, Irvin."

Raber nodded sternly. His fingers tightened on the reins. With ire, he said, "I've still got kids at risk. As if it weren't already bad enough, nobody has seen young Abe Yoder for over a week."

"Irvin, I'd like to talk to the other kids in Schlabaugh's gang. And we've got to find Sara."

"Some of the younger Yoder boys saw her drive off with two English."

"That's not quite right, Irvin, and I suspect you know it. What I heard the boys tell Miriam was that those men forced her car off the road and pushed her into the back of a white SUV. I phoned the sheriff immediately, and they'll have been looking for her all this time."

Raber shot Cal an alarmed look. Troyer held the bishop's gaze sternly.

Raber said, "You're right, Cal. I got pretty much the same story earlier."

Gently, Cal said, "Irvin, you've got to start trusting the law. You can't fix this on your own. It's too complicated."

Raber took the whip that was clipped to the side of the buckboard and tapped out a faster pace for his horse. "I didn't know what to do, Cal."

"It's a mistake to think that the law is always against you, Irvin."

"We are descended from those who were persecuted in the old countries, Cal. In our time, we will be persecuted, too, even in America. All our martyr hymns teach us to distrust secular authority."

"Sara has been abducted, Irvin," Cal said forcefully. "Sheriff Robertson is her best chance for a rescue."

Irvin groaned, "It's not that simple. We are devoted to self-sufficiency. To our separated lives. Letting the sheriff into our world cuts against the grain."

"You've got to start trusting people, Irvin," Cal said softly. "You need the help."

Raber implored, "How, Cal? Tell me how."

"For one thing," Cal said, "you could round up those kids. Under the circumstances, I doubt any of them would balk. You could tell them all to talk with the sheriff. Tell him everything they know that could help find Sara. Then you could get the Schlabaugh family, or one of those kids, to let the sheriff into John Schlabaugh's trailer back there."

"How'd it get to be this bad, Cal?

"Maybe your families have let the Rumschpringe go too far."

"Then that'd be my fault," the bishop said. "I hold the ultimate authority. You know that, Cal. But the kids have to be free to test the English world. Otherwise, they won't know for sure that they want to be Amish for the rest of their lives. They won't come to their faith through an honest repentance."

"Maybe they don't all need to see the world before they know they want to live Amish."

"It's not like we kick them out of a buggy in front of a town bar, Cal."

"I know. And I'm not saying you do. But now, you've got to accept some help. Trust the sheriff, Irvin. Start by helping us find Sara and Abe Yoder. We've wasted too much time as it is."

Friday, July 23
12:25 P.M.

RICKY NIELL was on foot, going from house to house in Saltillo, up on the high ridge. He had talked with almost a dozen people so far. Wives and grandfathers. Older children tending to their chores. A young woman cutting grass with a gas mower. An older fellow sitting on a porch bench. Everywhere, the story had been the same. Yes, John Schlabaugh was rebellious. No, they didn't know anything about Sara Yoder, or where she might be found. Kids on the Rumschpringe, you see, were pretty much left alone.

At the edge of town, he found a six-year-old boy in Dutch attire, perched on a white board fence. He sat silently, merely nodding his head as Ricky walked up. Tired from walking the hills, Ricky leaned back next to the lad to rest, both of them gazing out over the hills to the west.

Several minutes passed silently. Several awkward minutes for Ricky, who was used to at least a greeting. Eventually, Ricky adjusted to the moment. No need to talk. Sociable enough just to rest together on the fence.

The boy plucked a well-chewed straw from his mouth, tossed it into the grass at his feet, and pulled a fresh one from the pocket of his vest. He offered one to Niell, and Niell took it without comment. Together, for five minutes or so, they worried their straws around with their teeth, and occasionally spat out a sliver.

As he handed Niell a second fresh straw, the lad said, "Heaven's in a box."

Niell nodded, took the new straw in his teeth, and said, "How do you figure?"

"My cousin is dead, and they're gonna put him in a box."

"And?"

"And die Memme says good people go to heaven when they're dead."

Ricky said, "So heaven's in a box."

"In the ground."

Niell let a moment pass and then said, "Maybe they just put the body in the ground."

"Only place I've ever seen dead people is in a box."

"You ask your mom, but I'll bet she says the body goes in the ground, and the spirit goes to heaven."

"Then what's the spirit?"

"It's who you really are."

"The real me that's here is what I can touch. I'll go in a box someday, too."

"Can you touch your thoughts? Your dreams?"

"No."

"Aren't they the most important part of who you are?"

"I suppose. But, what I can touch is gonna go in a box. So, heaven's in a box."

"Is that what's going to happen to John Schlabaugh?"

"My daddy is making his box, now."

Ricky nodded, smiled. "Can all your memories fit in a box?"

"No."

"Can you think of anything else that won't fit in a box?"

After a spell, "Prayers."

"That's good. I like that."

"These things go to heaven?"

"They're called your spirit. It's all made up of who you really are. Your spirit."

"Is John Schlabaugh's spirit in heaven?"

"I believe so."

"Die Memme says he was bad."

"Maybe your mom didn't know everything about John Schlabaugh that God knows."

"My sister says he was fun."

"What's your sister's name?"

"Mary."

"What's your name?"

"Lester A. Troyer."

"Nice to meet you, Lester. I'm Ricky Niell."

Lester gave a satisfied nod of his head. "My sister knew John Schlabaugh very well."

"I'd like to talk to her."

"You should. She can tell you all about him."

"Is she home, today?"

"Naw."

"Do you know where she is?"

"My parents won't tell me. They say she's got a life of her own for a spell."

"If I came back later, would she be here?"

Lester popped off the fence, and turned to look at Niell. He shrugged, said, "I don't know," and added, "I'm not supposed to talk to strangers."

9

Friday, July 23
12:35 P.M.

IN Bruce Robertson's pine-paneled office, on the first floor of the red brick jail, Professor Branden sprawled in a low leather chair beside the sheriff's massive cherry desk. The comfort Branden usually felt in that soft chair eluded him, as he wrestled with the grim details of the case. With his head propped on the back of the chair, he gazed up at the ornate, hand-hammered tin ceiling tiles and brooded. It simply had never happened before. An Amish lad murdered this way.

Robertson sat upright, with his elbows propped on the desk. He had a pencil in his fingers, and had been drubbing the eraser impatiently against the resonant wood, trying, like Branden, to phrase the right questions. A pizza box lay open on the desk, the few remaining slices growing cold.

"It's not going to be a coincidence," Robertson said, "that Spits Wallace has old blood in his kitchen and we later find an Amish kid who's been dead a while."

"I don't think Spits is smart enough to make up such a good lie about that," Branden said. "About Abe and John being out there with English guys."

"He was smart enough to run us off his place," Robertson said.

"You going back after him?"

"He owes us another conversation, at the least. But I'm not going back out there until I know more about these Amish kids."

"He'd be hard to arrest under any circumstances," Branden observed.

"Yeah, but if he's not telling the truth, if he's involved in a drug deal with John Schlabaugh, for instance, then I'll need to coordinate with DEA before I try to take him down."

"And what if he is telling the truth?" Branden asked.

"I don't know. It's possible," Robertson said. "Dan would have known if Wallace's name is on the DEA list like Schlabaugh's is. So I'm not inclined to think Spits is involved with drugs."

"To me, he just doesn't seem like the type," Branden said. "Too much of a loner."

"I know. Wallace called them 'city slickers.'" Robertson said. "That doesn't sound like a hooked-up guy to me."

"No," Branden frowned. "But you're gonna have to devise a way to question him further without getting shot." He rubbed a paper napkin at his beard and said, "And if he's not involved, then it might mean that Abe and John had a falling out themselves. Argued over their drugs."

"And what?" Robertson asked. "Abe shot John?"

"Not likely," Branden conceded. "But something might have gone wrong when one or both of them hooked up with the wholesalers."

"And those wholesalers are the ones who grabbed up Sara Yoder?" Robertson offered.

"Cal definitely said Sara was abducted?"

"Yes. He was clear about that when he called. He said Miriam Yoder hadn't translated precisely when he and Ricky talked to her and some kids. He said the boys described some strangers forcing Sara into their car."

"So maybe those are the same people who were out at Spits Wallace's place with Yoder and Schlabaugh," Branden said, and shifted to a vertical position in his chair. He tossed the wadded napkin onto the lid of the pizza box. "Maybe that's the bunch from Columbus that Sara mentioned to Cal and me," he said.

"You buy the notion that Amish kids are that involved in hard drugs? More than just marijuana, I mean."

"Perhaps. She didn't elaborate," Branden said. "But she intimated that her gang of kids was into using drugs, though I can't say which ones. Could be anything, I suppose."

"Then try this," Robertson said. "Abe Yoder and John Schlabaugh were leading those 'city slickers' to Spits Wallace's gold."

Branden shrugged, got out of his chair, and paced in front of the large windows, looking west onto Clay Street at slow traffic making the turn onto Jackson. While he was there, Ellie came into the spacious office and said, "I'm going to start a fresh pot of coffee."

To the right of the office door, she worked at a credenza, emptying out the old grounds into a wastebasket, and said, "Ricky's coming in. There's nothing yet on Sara Yoder. Cal Troyer is taking a ride with the bishop to try to get some cooperation. Ricky doubled back, trying to get more of the details from the Amish kids who saw her taken away."

Ellie carried the carafe into the hall. She came in with fresh water in the pot, set up the drip basket, and switched the machine on. To the sheriff, she commented, "I know she's already eighteen or so, but maybe you ought to consider an Amber Alert."

Robertson eyed his dispatcher-secretary and nodded. He tossed his pencil into a can on his desk and said, "I know. But I'd like to wait until I've heard from the DEA people. Don't want to foul their nest."

Ellie countered, "Amish kids aren't ever drug dealers, Bruce. You're wasting time worrying about the DEA."

Robertson studied Ellie's determined expression and tapped out a drumbeat on his desk with his knuckles. "Look, Ellie," he said. "We've got one Amish kid shot through the head, and we've got another one grabbed by strangers in a white SUV. Sara herself told the professor, here, that Abe Yoder and John Schlabaugh had drug connections in Columbus. That's going to fall under a DEA taskforce concern. They've got a Mobile Enforcement Team working down there, and they've started an investigation up here. So I can't jump the gun on this one."

Ellie planted her fists on her hips and squared up to the sheriff's desk.

Branden smiled at her determination and said, "Maybe she's right, Bruce." He'd seen Ellie take on the big sheriff before.

She was in the habit of speaking more directly to the sheriff than most of the deputies did, especially when she disagreed with him, and she knew from long experience that he used his great bulk and gruff personality mainly as command tools. She also knew he listened to her when she took a stand on an issue. Calmly, she said, "Are you gonna make the call, or do I have to?"

The first genuine smile of the day appeared on Robertson's face. He rapped his knuckles on the desk again and said, "I'll have you do it, Ellie. Set it up ahead of time, and then I'll tell you when to release it to the press."

"That's better," Ellie said, and turned and walked out to her front desk down the hall.

Branden said, "She's right, Bruce."

Robertson faked ire, and couldn't hold the stern expression. Smiling, he shook his head and said, "One day I'm going to win an argument with that woman."

"You might as well just give her a raise, and get it over with," Branden said.

Cal Troyer came in from the outer hall and asked, "What's Ellie smiling about?"

Robertson grunted, and Branden said, "She won a face-off with our ponderous sheriff, here."

Cal looked back and forth between the two men. "Something I'd enjoy?" he asked.

"We're going to put out an Amber Alert on Sara Yoder," Robertson said.

"Good," Cal said, and took a seat in a straight-backed chair in front of Robertson's desk. "Irvin Raber just dropped me off. He's going to put his whole district at our disposal."

Branden asked, "Can he round up the other kids in Schlabaugh's group?"

"Says they'll all be in this afternoon."

"They're coming here?" Robertson asked.

"That's the plan."

Branden said, "Can he get us into Schlabaugh's place, Cal?"

"We can meet him out there today," Cal said. "Two o'clock. He told me where the place is."

The intercom buzzed and Ellie said over the crackle of the old system, "Ricky's here. He's been asking around out by Saltillo."

Robertson punched his intercom button and said, "Send him back, Ellie."

Ellie said, "You've also got Missy Taggert on line one."

Robertson picked up his phone, punched line one, and said, "What have you got, Missy?" and then listened to his wife, saying, "Right. Right. OK."

As he hung up, Niell came in and took a seat next to Cal in front of the cherry desk. Branden returned to his leather chair beside the desk.

Robertson said, "Missy's got Schlabaugh cleaned up. Says he was beat up pretty badly before he was shot. Also, he's got cocaine residue in his nostrils."

Niell whispered sarcastically, "Great."

Surprised, Cal asked, "She's sure?"

Robertson said, "It's Missy! Of course she's sure."

Cal tented his fingers in front of his lips and blew out tension with a slow whistle of air.

Ricky said to Cal, "What do you know about that 14/7 something with Abe Yoder?"

Cal took his tented fingers away from his lips and took a minute to clear his mind. "14/7," he repeated. "That's the financial arrangement some of the Amish families set up for older children who work away from the farm."

Robertson asked, "Does that have a bearing on this case?"

Ricky said, "The youngsters I talked to said old man Yoder had a 14/7 going with his son Abe Yoder, and Abe had gone sour on the deal."

Cal said, "It's not the best arrangement for the kids, if you only look at the financial side of the matter."

Branden said, "They work for room and board, right?"

"Something like that," Cal said. "A boy is considered old enough to hold a job at fourteen, sometimes younger. And he quits school at sixteen. Then, if he doesn't start a family after school, the father will get an agreement that says something like: 'You have lived in my house for fourteen years scot-free. Now, for half of that, the next seven years, if you stay on with us, then you go get a job, and whatever you make is rightfully mine.' The kid can stay on until age twenty-one or so, but everything he makes goes to the father, and by implication, to the family as a whole."

"You're kidding," Niell said. "I've lived here all my life and never heard about that before."

"Amish don't advertise it," Cal said. "But the way they see it, it's fourteen years free living as a kid. Seven years to pay it back as an adult. It builds family wealth."

Robertson said, "It makes you wonder how a young fella is supposed to get a start in life if everything he earns from fourteen to twenty-one goes to the father."

"Sometimes it's only half of what they earn," Cal qualified.

"Still," Niell said, "that stinks."

"When an Amish boy seeks to marry and join the church, everyone helps him out," Cal said. "Building a house. Arranging land. Wedding gifts. Everything he'll need to make a good start. The implied promise is that if you put all your worth into the family, the family in turn will stand by you when you need help. Any kind of help."

Branden asked Niell, "Abe Yoder didn't like his arrangement?"

Niell said, "Apparently not. I asked some of the neighbors out there. About a month ago, Abe quit his job at a print shop in Walnut Creek. Stayed away from the house a lot."

Branden asked, "Then where's he been staying? Out at John Schlabaugh's?"

Niell said, "Not from what the youngsters I talked to said. They think he's got a separate place somewhere."

Dan Wilsher knocked, entered the office, and said, "We've tracked down the owners of that barn. A retired couple up in Ashtabula, and they didn't know that Amish kids had been using it. Didn't even know that the barn was unlocked."

"What's the name of the owners?" Cal asked.

"Peterborough," Wilsher said. "A Jim and Nancy Peterborough."

"Remember those cabins?" Cal said.

"Cabins?" Wilsher asked.

Robertson said, "Jim Peterborough's dad deeded land over by those old strip mines to Mansfield for a summer camp for at-risk kids from the city. They built some cabins a while back, and ran a summer program for close to a dozen years there."

Branden said, "Is there anything still out there, Bruce?"

"If I remember correctly," Robertson said, "that's out on a looping road off 129. Spits Wallace lives about a half mile through the woods from there. As far as I know, the cabins are still there. Simple, one-story boxes, with tin roofs and brown wood siding. A couple of windows in each one, plus a bathroom, and kitchenette, and a small front porch. They're going to be pretty run down by now." He turned back to Wilsher. "Anything on the Firebird?"

"I've been through the trunk," Wilsher said. "I found some smoky English clothes, a ratty sleeping bag, some canned and boxed foods, and a box of videotapes."

"Pornography?" Robertson asked.

"I don't think so," Wilsher answered. "Not unless it's home-made stuff. No, these are the little tape cassettes that go in a video camera. Somebody has shot a bunch of videotape."

"So what's on them?" Robertson asked.

"I've got Carter watching them now. It'll take a few hours before I can tell you what we've got."

As he spoke, Robertson's phone rang. He picked up and said, "Yeah." Then, "OK, I understand. We won't mess in your game, Tony. But we want to go ahead with an Amber Alert on Sara Yoder. Like I told you, it's Sara we're most concerned about. Could be Columbus folk who grabbed her."

Robertson listened, scribbled a few notes on a yellow pad, said, "Good. I'll expect to hear from you if you see her down there. No, it's not routine at all. It's urgent. OK. Fine. I understand."

Robertson hung up, and through his intercom, he told Ellie, "Set up a press conference for three o'clock, Ellie. And post the Amber Alert to all Ohio sheriff and police departments. Use the state's system to get it out to everyone."

Ellie said, "The stroke of one key, Bruce. There, it's done."

Robertson said, "Thanks," and switched off. To the men in the room he declared, "Ellie just put that Amber Alert into effect. I'll announce it to the media at 3:00 P.M. Also, the DEA is going to put double surveillance on all their spots down in Columbus. Evidently Gahanna, too. Watch for Sara Yoder to turn up. Now, what's our next step?"

Niell said, "There's that Firebird to process. It looks like there's dried blood in the front seat."

Wilsher said, "I want the state BCI lab people to go through the Firebird."

Robertson nodded approval.

"Someone needs to go out to Schlabaugh's place at two o'clock," Cal said. "Mike and I can handle that."

Robertson turned questioning eyes to the professor.

Branden said, "I'll meet you at the Schlabaugh place, Cal, if you can give me directions."

Cal nodded.

"In the meantime," Branden said, "I think I know where to go hunting for Abe Yoder."

"OK. Just fill me in before you leave. But listen up, everybody. Sara Yoder is the priority here. Dan, I want everybody we've got out looking for her. Call in the night-shift people. Everybody goes out. We'll have to trust DEA to cover Columbus spots, but if she's still in Holmes County, I don't want to hear later that we missed her for lack of trying. It's been nearly three hours since she was abducted, and I don't want to hear that we've found her dead in a ditch somewhere."

10

Friday, July 23
1:15 P.M.

PROFESSOR Branden drove up onto the college heights to his home, where he changed into hiking boots and a long-sleeved khaki shirt. While drinking a quick cup of coffee with his wife in their kitchen, he told Caroline about the events of the morning and the pressing search for Sara Yoder, both in Holmes County by sheriff's deputies and in Columbus by DEA agents operating an undercover investigation there. He gulped the last of his coffee, pushed back his chair, saying, "Got to get going," and headed for the hall to the garage.

Caroline sprang up to block him. She stood nearly an inch taller, and resolutely faced him down. "You can take time for some lunch, Michael."

She reckoned that he hadn't told her half the important details in the case. She also knew the danger he sometimes put himself in, and she intended this morning to know his plans before he left. So she pushed up against him, hands on his shoulders, and moved him back to his kitchen chair.

When he was reseated there, smiling but giving no indication that he would jump up again, she put a box of saltines, a jug of milk with two glasses, and a jar of peanut butter with a table knife on the curly maple tabletop, and spread peanut butter on one of the crackers. She handed it to him and spread one for herself.

Branden ate the cracker, poured two glasses of milk, and said, "I thought I'd go looking for Abe Yoder."

Caroline brushed her long auburn hair behind her ears and said, "Why wouldn't you help look for Sara?"

"Everybody else is already doing that. In the meantime, I'm supposed to meet Cal Troyer and Bishop Rader at the murdered boy's trailer at two o'clock."

"John Schlabaugh?"

"Right. It's Schlabaugh who is dead. Abe Yoder has been missing for a week or so, and Sara Yoder was abducted this morning. There was trouble, like I told you, at Spits Wallace's place a week ago, so there's a connection there somehow. Wallace said Abe and John had a run-in at his house with some 'city slickers' in a white SUV. Today, Sara was driven off by two English men in a white SUV. It's all related, somehow. So, I figure finding Abe Yoder is, at this point, every bit as important as finding Sara Yoder. If he's still alive."

Caroline eyed her husband, handed over another peanut butter cracker, and said, "Lawrence Mallory was here today, looking for you."

"He's drafting another one of our papers on the siege of Atlanta."

"He said you wanted this one finished by the start of fall semester, and you had worked on the draft only once."

"I'll get to it after this case wraps up."

"And Arne Laughton called. He says your committee on the Favor estate owes him another report."

Branden grinned, then drank some milk, eyes laughing.

"What's so funny, Professor?"

"He's worried that I'll allocate more money for the sciences."

"That's going to be a problem for you?"

"Not a problem for me. But for him, yes, when classes start. He'll have a dozen unhappy professors in his office. In the meantime, I've got this case with Robertson, and that's what I'm going to work on."

Caroline knew better than to try to talk him out of it. She spread peanut butter, ate a cracker, and remembered the dozen or so cases for which the professor's involvement as a sheriff's reserve deputy had made the difference in the sheriff's investigation. She had wondered, sometimes, who was helping whom. Were they Robertson's cases, or Branden's? The men had known each other since grade school. Bruce Robertson, Cal Troyer, and Michael Branden. Compared to that, she was a latecomer in the professor's life. She wasn't insecure about that, but she did recognize the pull each man had on the others' lives. Working together when Amish were involved because Cal knew the Amish and because Branden and Robertson thinking together always added up to more than twice what each could accomplish alone. Holmes County's famous threesome. Her husband's identity was defined here as much as at the college where he taught.

Gazing across the table, Caroline recognized the impatient attitude in his posture and expression. She handed him a last cracker, and said, "Just be careful, Michael."

※　※　※

Branden took his truck back out County 58 to 129, and followed the map Cal Troyer had made for him to the old cabins on the property bordering the Spits Wallace place.

The road looped around a tall stand of old pines, and came back in front of the cabins, locked in a tangle of new-growth trees. Seeing a path worn through tall ferns in front of the third cabin, Branden parked there, and mounted the steps to the weathered front porch. He pushed on the door and heard a clatter at the back of the cabin, then someone crashing through the bushes behind the cabins. He thought he heard an anxious voice inside the cabin, and he rattled the doorknob. There was a thump as if something heavy had hit the floorboards. He moved to the window beside the door, looked in, and saw a work boot and a leg in denim trousers lying on the floor beside the foot of an old, sagging bed.

At the door, he took hold of the knob and threw his shoulder against the old wood. Part of the doorjamb cracked and splintered, and he stepped back and kicked the door in. As he crossed the threshold, the first thing that assaulted him was the odor of rotting flesh.

On the floor, he found a boy in Amish clothes, with a scruffy Vandyke beard and mustache, in a bloody shirt, lying prone on the old linoleum, trying to lift a black revolver from the floor to point it at the door Branden had splintered. Branden advanced quickly, kicked the gun loose, and picked it up. It was sticky, and when he pulled his hand away from the grip, he saw blood on his fingers and palm.

He put the gun on the kitchen table, knelt beside the boy, felt his forehead, pushed himself upright, and stepped outside. He wiped the blood off his hand with a handkerchief and called Ellie down at the jail.

"Ellie, I'm gonna need an ambulance out at the old Peterborough cabins."

Ellie answered, "I'll roll a squad right away."

"It's a young Amish kid," Branden said. "He's barely conscious. And I think he's been shot."

"Can you give me more for the squad, Mike? His condition?"

"Hang on," Branden said and stuffed the phone into his shirt pocket.

Back in the cabin, Branden turned the now-unconscious boy onto his back and unbuttoned his blood-soaked shirt. In the lad's left side, there was an ugly wound, surrounded by a hideous bruise, oozing a thin stream of blood. Across the circular wound, there were several black threads sewn into the skin. Most of them had torn loose, and all were crusted with blood.

Branden checked his breathing and left him where he was, while he made a fast search of the cabin. There was a kerosene lantern on an old round table, and the floor was littered with empty cans and cast-off wrappers and boxes from fast-food chains.

At each of the small windows, he pulled back tattered curtains to admit more light, and then he knelt again beside the boy and turned him onto his side. He lifted the shirttail and found another wound at the lad's back, near the left kidney.

Outside, Branden fished his cell back out of his pocket and said, "He's been shot, Ellie. In at the back left, and out at the left side, front. He's been here a while. There are food scraps from several days, anyway. Breathing is shallow, temperature high, and there's a bad odor to the wound."

Ellie said, "I got that, Doc. The squad is on its way. I'll relay everything to them."

"Tell them to run with full sirens, Ellie. I want whoever is out here to know they are coming. I don't want anyone thinking they have time to come back and jump me."

"Full sirens, Mike."

"Good, now can you get me Bruce?"

Immediately, Robertson said, "I'm right here at Ellie's desk, Mike. How long's he been there?"

Branden said, "Couple of days, anyway. Probably more like a week. The place is full of garbage. Old meals, and empty cans and wrappers. And I think he tried to sew himself up."

Ellie said, "My guys should be there soon. You hear any sirens?"

Branden said, "Faintly. OK, yeah, that's them coming up the hill. Ellie, tell them the access road loops around some pines and comes in through a dense tangle of trees, west of the cabins. I'm in the third one."

Back in the cabin, Branden tried to rouse the boy, talk to him. When the paramedics climbed onto the front porch and clumped into the room, Branden was cradling the boy's head in one hand, the other palm taking the temperature of the forehead.

The paramedics moved Branden aside quickly. They took vitals, hooked up an IV line, and had the boy loaded into the ambulance before Branden could tell them anything of significance. When the ambulance was headed back down the access road,

Branden's cell phone rang and Robertson said, "They have him loaded up yet?"

"They're on their way back into town."

"Good, Mike. I'm on my way, too. You stay put. I'm coming up 129, now. I'll be out there in two minutes."

* * *

Robertson pulled around to the front, parked his black-and-white unit behind the professor's truck, and got out and climbed up to the porch. He called out, "Mike!" and Branden answered from behind the cabin. Robertson bounded down the steps and circled around through tall weeds to the back of the cabin, where he saw Branden studying a pushed-out screen over the window of the cabin's bathroom.

Branden pulled the screen loose and said, "When I knocked, someone punched out through this screen and ran off through the woods, there."

Robertson paced off a few steps along a narrow path in the weeds, came to the edge of dense woods, and said, "We're not going to be able to track anyone here."

Branden led the sheriff around the cabin to the front porch, and the two men climbed the steps. Inside, Robertson kicked his toe through some of the refuse on the floor, and then saw the table and the gun lying on it.

"He had a gun, Mike?" Robertson asked.

Branden said, "Yes, I took it from him."

"Do we know who he is?"

"He's about the right age to be Abe Yoder. And his beard is cut to a fancy trim, typical of a rebellious kid on the Rumschpringe."

Robertson stood beside him and asked, "Did he point that gun at you?"

"Not really. He was too weak to lift it."

"Amish don't use handguns, Mike."

"Sheriff, it appears that maybe one of them does."

"Let's search the place," Robertson said, and turned back into the cabin.

In the kitchenette, there were old pans and metal dinner plates in the sink. In the one cupboard, there was an old jar of freeze-dried coffee and a flour sack, split open along the bottom seam. In the corner beside the bed stood an old, pressed-board suitcase with its handle torn off. It was tied shut with cotton twine. When they had it untied, they opened it on the bed and found Amish clothes, male, fairly new. Under the bed, they found several bloody towels.

Robertson's cell phone rang, and he stepped outside and down the steps of the porch to answer it. Dan Wilsher reported that Deputy Carter had found something interesting on the videotapes: John Schlabaugh taking a briefcase from a tall, redheaded man.

Branden came out on the porch, saying, "Bruce, look here."

Robertson switched off and turned to see Branden holding an old-fashioned, hinged leather briefcase.

Branden said, "It was stuck up behind the sink, under the counter."

Robertson knelt with Branden on the rough boards of the porch to open the briefcase. Inside, they found a thick bundle of twenty-dollar bills and a large plastic bag of white powder. Another bag held gray tablets imprinted with the emblem of a shooting star.

Robertson said, poking the bag, "That's gonna be cocaine. And the tablets? Dollars to doughnuts that's Ecstasy. The big X, Mike. These boys were into real trouble, big time, let me tell ya."

11

Friday, July 23
2:00 P.M.

CAL TROYER drove Bishop Raber to John Schlabaugh's place in the Doughty Valley, expecting to meet Professor Branden there. When Raber indicated the driveway, Cal pulled his work truck in beside a battered single-wide mobile home on a yellow concrete-block foundation set close to the road. Next to the rusty home, about twenty paces down a dirt lane, a tall gray barn stood on level ground in the deep shade of a stand of old hickory trees, which had peppered the barn and ground with dead branches and cast-off bark.

Raber said, jingling keys on a ring, "We can start in the barn. I got these from young Andy Stutzman. He says at least three of the fellas have keys to the place. To store their cars."

At the barn, Raber unlocked a new, shiny padlock on a heavy metal hasp and pulled one of the corrugated metal doors around and back against the barn's left front. Cal matched him on the right, and afternoon sun streamed into the structure, sparkling through a light haze of suspended dust. A flutter of wings in the peak brought a flock of startled pigeons out into the open air.

Inside the barn, in dim light to the right, there were two cars parked with their front ends pointed out. A cotton dustcloth haphazardly covered the windshield and roof of one of the cars. In the center of the barn stood an old green and yellow John Deere tractor, and behind that there was an assortment of farm implements, most showing rust.

Raber stared at the tractor distastefully, lifted his eyebrows, and let out a long sigh. "To think that such a machine could cause so much trouble," he whispered.

Cal pulled the dust cover off the one car, a dull yellow Ford Escort, and climbed in on the passenger side. He opened the glove box, sorted through some papers, read a name on the registration, and asked, "John Miller?"

"That's one of them," Raber said.

In the other car, a white Chevy Nova from the '60s, Cal found the registration papers and said, "I know this fellow. Lives down the valley. Jeremiah Miller."

Raber smiled wanly and said, "That's one of the boys who want to marry Sara Yoder."

"He's not in your district," Cal said. "He's with the Melvin Miller congregation."

Raber shrugged. "The kids all know each other these days. Ten miles is only a ten-minute ride for them, anymore. It'd take an hour in a buggy."

Cal's phone rang, and he stepped outside to take the call. As he listened, he waved Raber over to him, said, "OK, Mike," and switched off.

Intently, Cal said, "Irvin, they've found a young man, hurt, and Mike thinks it may be Abe Yoder. They're at Pomerene Hospital."

*   *   *

Cal pulled in under the carport at the emergency room doors, let the bishop out on the blacktop, and backed up into a parking space at Joel Pomerene Memorial Hospital, on a steep hill beside the Wooster Road. In the lobby, they found Mike Branden and Bruce Robertson talking with a doctor in green scrubs. As they walked up, the doctor was saying, tying on a scrub hat, "I don't think it nicked the kidney. It's the infection I'm worried about."

Branden introduced the doctor to Raber, and the bishop followed the doctor to one of the curtained rooms. When he came out, Raber stated, "It's Abe Yoder, all right."

Cal said, "We need to get Albert and Miriam Yoder to come in."

"They're taking him into surgery," Robertson said. "Going to clean out the wound."

Raber asked, "How long could that take, do you think?"

Robertson said, "Depends."

Raber asked, "Does anyone know how bad off he is?"

Branden said, "He tried to stitch himself up several days ago. The infection has had a long time to fester."

"He could die?" Raber asked.

None of the three English men volunteered an answer.

Cal cleared his throat and said, "Irvin, do you know their cell phone number?"

Raber shook his head and turned to go back to where the nurses were working to prepare Yoder for surgery. Cal laid a hand on his arm and pulled him gently back around. "Don't worry about it, Irvin. Ricky Niell wrote their numbers down," Cal said, and let the distracted bishop go.

Robertson said, "I'll call Niell," and stepped outside to call the jail.

Branden stopped a nurse in pink scrubs and asked, "Can we talk to him?"

The nurse said, "He hasn't been conscious. We've sedated him now for surgery."

Down the hall, an orderly pushed Abe Yoder's gurney out into the hall, and then into the elevator while a doctor held the doors open. As Yoder rolled by, Bishop Raber reached out and gave his hand a gentle squeeze. When the elevator doors closed, the nurses and orderlies in the emergency room went quietly and efficiently about their other duties.

Cal watched Irvin Raber take it all in with a stunned look on his face, and the pastor said to him, gently, "The sheriff will have Sergeant Niell contact the Yoders and bring them into town, Irvin."

Raber blinked and looked at Cal and then Branden in turn. "It suffices to know that he is alive," he said. "He's been in God's hands since the day he was born."

*   *   *

When Albert P. and Miriam Yoder arrived, they were dressed in formal Sunday attire. Albert P. wore a black suit with a plain waist-coat, and Miriam wore a long, dark green dress with a white lace bodice. He was in a black felt hat, she in a black bonnet. Bishop Raber got up from a waiting-room chair and took them aside. He spoke solemn Dutch at some length, and then the Yoders took seats next to each other in the waiting room. Beyond the few words they spoke to Raber, the Yoders said nothing. The cast of their eyes seemed to be at once purposeful and resigned.

Cal whispered a few words to Branden, and the professor stepped outside to stand under the carport with Robertson and Niell, letting Cal take the lead with the Yoders. Cal came outside after speaking a few words of encouragement to the Yoders, and asked Niell, "How'd they take it?"

Niell said, "Shocked. Like anybody would be, I guess. Also, glad that he's still alive."

Branden asked, "None of the kids came with them?"

"They've all got their orders, Doc," Niell said. "Chores and such. I couldn't get them here any faster. Mrs. Yoder took the time to speak to each one of the kids. Wouldn't leave any sooner."

Cal asked, "Did you tell them much about what happened? Explain how bad he is?"

Niell said, "Only what I know myself, and that isn't much."

Robertson said, somewhat bemused, "You notice they took the time to dress formal? You'd think they could have gotten here faster."

"Just being conservative," Cal said. "Amish don't panic readily."

To Branden he said, "You found him in one of the old Peterborough cabins?"

"Right," Branden said. "There was someone with him who ran off when I got there. I think he's been there since the trouble at the Spits Wallace place."

"Hiding from whom?" Cal asked.

Robertson said, "Look, Cal, it was always heading this way with the Rumschpringes. Sooner or later. Now two kids have gotten themselves shot over drugs, and the whole bunch of them is tied up in it. For all I know, one of them shot the other!"

"That's just baloney," Cal growled, muscles tensing in his arms and neck.

Robertson said, "They're going to account for themselves, and I'm not waiting any longer. Every hour puts Sara Yoder at greater risk."

Branden said, "Good luck rounding them up," and got a scowl from the sheriff.

Cal said, "They've all agreed to an interview at 6:00."

Robertson said, "I don't think I can wait that long under the circumstances." To Niell, Robertson continued, "Ricky, bring them in. Any of them that you can round up. Just bring 'em in."

"Wait," Cal said. "I'll go back in and talk to Raber. Maybe he can get them together faster."

Cal left and Branden said, "There's still going to be plenty left to do."

Robertson said, "It's the weekend coming up, Mike. That'll stall us out."

Niell said, "The state BCI lab people aren't going to go through the Pontiac until Monday, anyway."

Robertson said, "OK. What else have we got?"

Branden volunteered, "Cal and I can still go out to Schlabaugh's trailer. I have the keys now. We could do that before we talk with the kids."

Robertson nodded approval.

"You'll also want to go through that cabin," the professor said. "See what we missed."

Robertson nodded again.

Niell asked, "What has Wilsher gotten off the phone dump?"

"Still working on it," Robertson said. "And Carter is screening more videotapes."

"Someone should try to talk to Abe Yoder when he wakes up," Cal said, as he walked up to the men. "Irvin is using the Yoders' cell phone. Might be his first time doing that. Anyway, he says he'll have them all here by four o'clock at the latest."

"He can do that?" Niell asked.

"He's the bishop," Cal said flatly.

When Robertson and Niell had headed for their car, Cal said to Branden, "Mike, one of the cars in Schlabaugh's barn belongs to someone we know."

Branden waited.

"You saved his life when he was ten."

"Jeremiah Miller?"

"He's the one who wants to marry Sara Yoder."

12

Friday, July 23
2:45 P.M.

AT John Schlabaugh's trailer, Cal's gray work truck was parked
back by the barn, under the tall hickory trees. Branden found Cal
and Bishop Irvin Raber going through the trunk of the yellow
Escort parked inside the barn. As sunny as the afternoon was, the
light was dim in the barn, and Troyer and Raber were working
with a flashlight.

When Branden arrived, Cal said, "Hold these, Mike," and
handed Branden a tangle of English clothes smelling strongly of
stale cigarette smoke and beer. Branden laid the clothes across
a wooden sawhorse that stood against the interior wall of the
barn.

Next, Cal pulled out an assortment of camping gear, and handed
the items one at a time to Branden, who stacked the goods on the
concrete pad, behind the parked cars. In Branden's stack there was
a sleeping bag of green nylon and a green Coleman lantern in a red
plastic case. A small hatchet. An aluminum cook kit of nested pans
and skillets, banded together with a loop of copper wire. Fishing
tackle. A folding chair. And last, a GPS receiver like the one they
had found in John Schlabaugh's grave. Branden switched it on and
found the batteries dead.

Cal observed, "This is John Miller's car, Mike. He's one of the
kids in Schlabaugh's gang."

In a cardboard box pushed to the back of the trunk, Irvin Raber found a collection of pornographic magazines. He dropped the box back into the trunk as if it were a palpable evil and muttered to himself, something in dialect that Cal didn't understand.

Cal said, "It's pretty much the same thing in the Chevy, Mike," tipping his head at Jeremiah Miller's car.

Branden walked over to the tractor, studied the farm implements, and asked Raber, "This all belong to John Schlabaugh?"

Raber said, "Some of the men helped to pay for the plow and the reaper. The rest is John's."

At the trailer, out beside the road, Raber tried the keys and got the right one on the third try. Inside, they found a jumbled mess. Curtains torn from the windows, books strewn about on the floor. Dishes pulled down from the cupboards and shattered. Kitchen table upended, and balanced at an acute angle in the corner. Appliances tossed into a heap on the kitchen floor. A TV screen broken and the glass gouged out onto the carpet. Overturned ashtrays. Clothing emptied out of drawers. Bed off its frame, sheets and blankets crumpled and tossed into a corner.

Branden crunched through broken glass and turned the kitchen table upright. He set the two chairs beside it. Cal walked back to the bedroom and started sorting through the clothes that had been pulled from the drawers. Bishop Raber cleared a spot on the couch and sat down wearily.

Branden said, "It's been searched, Cal."

Cal came into the living room, studied the disarrayed electronics there, and said, "There used to be a computer here."

Raber gave a sorrowful moan, got up and sat on one of the chairs at the kitchen table. Cal joined him there, and Branden leaned back against the sink, arms folded over his chest. Raber cradled his head in his hands and began to talk softly.

"They've got everything they need, Cal, our kids. Homes, families, security. They've got it all, and still it's not enough. They've got an itch to scratch. So they scratch."

"They could make plenty of money and just stay home. It's not like we don't let them take jobs. Even with a 14/7, they lack for nothing.

"But that's where they get into trouble, on the jobs. Computers and phones. TVs and videos. It's all out there for them, the English world. Who can stop it? And it's been getting worse every year.

"And if, when they are young, we haven't managed to give them a faith that will sustain them, they are lost to the world when they leave us. Which one of us, without our faith, could hold to righteousness in this vain and faithless world?

"They see the glitter, those young ones. Sparkle and shine. But it's false. I know what's on those TVs, Cal. Glitter to snare the eye, and it's the eyes that are the windows to the souls of the boys. They want what they see, and nowadays, they see it all.

"So, how do we keep them home, Cal? How do we keep them safe? If they have to see the world, then we must prepare them to see the truth. To see the rust beneath the glitter, before it is too late.

"So, I preach the Word, Cal, let me tell you. They all know what the Good Book says. We preach commitment to the only real thing there is—community. The church as the community of believers. We say to them, Stay! In the name of God, Stay! Forsake the world of golden streamers and glitter stars, where all is false and shallow. Stay, we say. Build a plain and simple life of commitment and community. Serve the Lord where you live. Live the life of sacrifice, devoted to the higher purposes. Live in the light, for God is light. Live in truth, for God is truth.

"And still they have to see the world for themselves, Cal. They don't know what my words signify until they've gotten themselves locked away for a drunken brawl or a stolen car. Alone is where the heart first cries out for touch, for communion, for belonging.

"I tell you the world has a ripping wind, Cal. It tears our children from our arms. They don't know the danger. We can't hold them. If they are ripped away, who can save them? If they falter alone, who is to mourn? And it's the Rumschpringe that lures them into the world. It has been a tradition for as long as any of us can remember, but I rue the day we ever allowed this Rumschpringe among us.

"But, without the Rumschpringe, who can know? Without the going, who can return? How will they know the truth of what we preach? Tell me it's not wrong, Cal, to let them go out into the world. Oh, if I could only know peace in this.

"Without the training of the church, how can they see the difference between good and evil? I tell you that they can't, Cal. They can't see. They have no sight at that age. And what can I do? I am only a bishop. What could I possibly know about the world? I, who have never tasted it, seen it, lived it. In my day, the Rumschpringe was a mild thing. A mere dalliance. 'How can I know?' they will say. I was called to be bishop when I was only forty-six. What did I know then? How can a man prepare for such a burden? The children come to me for answers. They want to know what the things mean that they see on television. What they mean, the things that they read in magazines. Lord, what can I know of these choices? What answers can I give? All I can do is uphold the Word and pray that it still has the power to preserve. To guide them when they are away from home. What else can I do?

"And what is happiness? How can a child of eighteen or twenty know what sorrows come streaming in on the winds? How can they see the glitter for what it really is? We say, 'Marry and raise a family.' The world says girls, girls, girls, and boys, boys, boys, on every street corner. Free love. Free sex. No commitments. And then it drops them into a lonely hole from which they can never escape. A loneliness that has no balm. Chasing the glitter stars from town to town. When all along they could have lived with real beauty, with God's family.

"These young ones don't know what terrible storms there are when they set out in their Rumschpringes. They only know temptation, mistaking it for love. Or thrills, mistaking them for security.

"So, that's why we've had a good Amish boy living here by himself, in a trailer. Surrounded by gadgets. Unspeakably alone. Dead.

"And a gang of kids running wild. Shot and killed. Laid up in the hospital. Young girls pulled into cars by ruffians. Parents with unspeakable grief.

"They need answers, too, these parents. It makes me want to cry out. They see their children drive off, and all I can tell them is to pray. Love them every minute you have, and pray without ceasing. Pray that the world won't drag them away. Pray that the children turn back and see the truth. Pray, sometimes, that they'll just make it home tonight, Lord. Pray that the sheriff never comes to your door in the middle of the night with the kind of news that rends your very heart from your chest. Like the news the Schlabaughs got this morning."

Raber took his hands away from his eyes and found that he had been weeping. He pressed the heels of his hands against his eye sockets and moaned. Cal had a handkerchief laid out on the table, and Raber took it gratefully and dried his eyes and blew his nose. He looked up at the professor and shrugged an apology. Shaking his head, he whispered, "I don't think I can bear the pain, if we don't find Sara Yoder in time."

13

Friday, July 23
4:00 P.M.

BRANDEN met Ricky Niell in the long hall on the first floor of Millersburg's cubical red brick jail, and they poked their heads into Interview A and Interview B. In each room, Robertson had set out a pitcher of water and a stack of paper cups. Placards on the gray metal tables admonished NO SMOKING. Each room held precisely four chairs, three at one end of the rectangular tables, and one by itself, at the other end.

In the sheriff's office, Robertson skipped pleasantries and said, "Look, it's critical that we get a line on where Sara Yoder is. The rest can wait. We know they're into drugs, and we can always come back to that later, if we really want an investigation. We don't know who shot John Schlabaugh, but if it was one of them, they won't be likely to own up to it today."

"It could just as likely be Spits Wallace who shot Abe and John, both," Branden said.

"Or Abe Yoder shot Schlabaugh," Niell suggested.

Branden shook his head and said, "Not Amish, Ricky. It's just not possible. Besides, who shot Abe, then? He was shot in the back. It would seem more likely to me that Spits shot one or even both of them."

Robertson punched his intercom button and said, "Ellie, where's Deputy Carter?"

"He's out with Captain Newell," Ellie answered. "They're checking bars in Wooster."

"Did he ever finish watching those videotapes?"

"Yes, and he marked one for you to see. Said it looked like a drug buy, involving John Schlabaugh and a big redheaded guy. Handing over a briefcase."

Robertson switched off and said, "If that's true, then the DEA can probably tell us who the redheaded guy is."

Again, Robertson punched the intercom. "Ellie, who've we got in the house right now?"

"Lieutenant Wilsher should be in the squad room, suiting up. Everyone else is out on patrol, or working the cell blocks."

Robertson stepped down the hall to the squad room, brought Wilsher back, and asked, "What'd you get from Abe Yoder's phone, Dan?"

Wilsher sat to finish tying a shoe and said, "It's all just regular calls, I think. Regular text messages. You know, 'Party tonight,' that sort of thing, with GPS coordinates."

"Nothing we can use?" Robertson asked, standing behind his desk.

Wilsher stood up and said, "Maybe one thing. Abe Yoder got a message from John Schlabaugh, using those number codes. It gives a time, 4:30 P.M., almost three weeks ago, now, and a GPS location down east of Columbus."

"We ought to get that location pinned down," Branden said.

"I've got Stan Armbruster working on that now," Wilsher said.

"OK, then we've got these interviews," Branden said. "If Ricky and I work in Interview A, then who'll be in Interview B?"

"That's Ellie and me," Robertson said. "I want her to take notes and also record the sessions. I've got the night shift dispatcher, Ed Hollings, coming in on overtime to handle the front desk for Ellie. We'll see each of the kids first, and play it serious and formal. Sheriff's investigation. Official capacity. That sort of thing. Then I want to send them in, one at a time, to see you and Ricky."

"And we operate casually," Ricky said.

"Right," said Robertson. "I want them to feel like they can open up to you. So, get them talking. Maybe they'll think the official interview is over, and relax."

"What are you going to ask them?" Branden asked.

"Official-sounding questions," Robertson said. "'Are you now using, or have you ever used, illegal drugs?' 'Do you know of anyone who has used illegal drugs?' 'Are you now involved, or have you ever been involved, in an illegal enterprise to grow, make, distribute, or sell illegal drugs?' Like that."

Branden grimaced. He studied the sheriff's stern expression and said, "By the time they get to us, they'll be too scared to talk."

"About drugs, yes," Robertson said. "But I want you to 'good cop' them into talking about what we really want."

"We're after a location," Branden said.

Robertson nodded. "Like I said, the other matters can wait. What we need, and I mean right now, is somewhere to look for Sara Yoder."

"You don't think the Amber Alert is going to produce any usable results, do you?" Ricky said.

"It's too soon to tell, but probably not," Robertson said. "DEA is a better bet for us, because if English took her, it's likely to be Columbus guys who did it. Because of the drug connection. Once we get something out of these kids, we'll push DEA for an action. Information. Something."

Ellie buzzed through on the intercom and said, "They're here, Sheriff."

"OK, gentlemen," Robertson said, and installed Branden and Niell in Interview A.

* * *

Robertson stepped down the hall to Ellie's reception counter. He came out through the swinging gate into the vestibule and shook Bishop Raber's hand. Then he counted heads and said, "You're short one, Bishop."

Raber replied evenly, "One of the lads is not in my district. He said he would be here, but . . . ," and he shrugged.

Robertson looked at the kids, each one in turn, and then said, "Who's to be first?"

Raber got all of the kids settled on benches in the vestibule and said, "Mary Troyer wants to be first."

A girl at the end of one of the benches stood up. She was dressed in her Sunday best, with black hose and new black shoes. Her aqua dress was long and pleated, and her bodice was gray. The strings of her black prayer cap fell untied over her shoulders. When she took a hesitant step forward, Robertson told her, using an officious tone, to write her name in a ledger on Ellie's counter. Nervously, the girl followed Robertson down to Interview B, and Ellie came last, with a steno pad.

In Interview B, down the hall on the left, across from the squad room, Robertson asked Mary Troyer his questions. That done, Ellie showed her into Interview A.

*　*　*

When Mary Troyer came into Interview A, she looked at her choice of chairs, and chose, without hesitating, to sit in the near chair, next to Branden and Niell. She sat with straight posture, hands folded in her lap, waiting for Branden or Niell to speak.

Branden said, "I am Professor Michael Branden, and this is Ricky Niell."

Niell was in street clothes, blue slacks and a white shirt and dark blue tie. His sport coat was hung casually over the back of his chair.

Mary said, "I am Mary Troyer," and did not question either man's credentials.

Branden said, "How'd it go with the sheriff, Mary?"

"I don't know," Mary said. "OK, I guess. I don't use drugs anymore. That's what I told the sheriff."

"Do you have any questions for us?" Niell asked.

"No. I guess not. We're trying to find Sara Yoder, aren't we? I told Mr. Robertson what I could, which isn't much, really, but I did what I could. Bishop Raber wants me to tell you everything."

"Have you known Sara long?" Branden asked.

"All my life. She lives near me."

"Out by Saltillo?" Branden asked casually.

"Just over the hill from there. My house is on 68, out past Gypsy Springs School."

"I guess you know her pretty well, then," Branden said. "Do you know all the kids out that way, or just the ones you pal around with?"

"We all go to school together. Or we did. Some of us are out of school now."

"Sara told us that there are nine kids in John Schlabaugh's group," Branden said.

"I wouldn't say I am part of anyone's special group," Mary told Branden.

"No," Branden said. "You're right. But some of the kids who live out your way use cell phones now, and Sara told me those are the nine kids who run with Schlabaugh."

"Well, if that's what you mean, then yes. But I don't like drugs. John Schlabaugh wants everybody to like drugs."

"Well, he did, anyway," Branden said.

Mary looked at her hands in her lap. "I'm sorry he's dead. You can believe that, for sure. But, I didn't mix in with his drugs."

"Was it just marijuana?" Branden asked.

"At first," Mary said. "One of the guys got some seeds. Grew some pot. We tried it. I don't like it. We're all different, Mr. Branden. I make my own decisions."

Branden nodded, smiled. "I like the way you said that, Mary."

"I'm not trying to be square. I just don't like the way pot makes me feel."

"Was Sara that way, too?"

"She smoked enough, I guess. Everybody does a little, one time or another, don't they? Then, John got something new. X or something. I just never got to the point where I liked it."

"That's probably Ecstasy, Mary. Did Sara like it?"

"I guess. She likes one of the boys, and he does some Ecstasy. She does, too, I guess. She went to Columbus once with John Schlabaugh. To see about getting some more."

Ricky sat up straighter and asked, "Do you know where in Columbus?"

"No," Mary said. "Sara never said. But she seemed worried after that. Like something in Columbus scared her pretty badly. That's when she started pulling back. Fewer parties. Seemed kind of distracted."

Branden asked, "Was Sara going to quit the Rumschpringe, Mary?"

"I don't know. She just seemed more standoffish. Like she was having doubts. But she likes one of the boys, so that probably kept her in it some."

"Is it Jeremiah Miller she likes?"

"Yes."

"They're pretty serious, Jeremiah and Sara?"

"I guess. She would do just about anything for him."

"Oh?"

"All the boys want sex. That's pretty normal. And our parties get to be wild, sometimes. But, I figure, ten years from now, I'm going to be living right here with the rest of them. How am I going to feel about things, then, if I sleep around now? It's not like I'm going to move to China."

"But you do go to the parties?"

"Everybody likes to have a little fun, Mr. Branden."

Branden waited for Mary to explain.

Mary said, "I'm probably going to have ten kids. I can see that, just looking around. It's OK to have a little fun before you marry. It's your only chance. But I don't get smashed like the boys."

"But, Mary, there are evidently drugs as well as alcohol at your parties."

"There's only a few who really want the drugs. The other kids just go along. Experiment a little. Mostly everybody just gets drunk. Sleeps it off. But I don't do the drugs. Don't want my babies to have birth defects. Nobody does."

"Did John and Abe always have the drugs, or is that a recent thing?"

"John has been talking a lot lately about cocaine. You know, coke. You sniff it in your nose. He got enough, somehow, so he could sell it around. He and Abe were pretty strong on that stuff. But not everybody was. Not me, anyways."

"You seem pretty reasonable about it."

"It's not like *I* can move to Kansas."

"What do you mean?"

"To get married. My parents want to drive me up to Middlefield. We have relatives there, and they know an Amish man who wants to get married. They want me to meet him. But that's just up to Middlefield. Henry Erb, now, he wants to move to Kansas. But he can do that. He's got a car, and his folks let him keep the money he earns. He can do anything he wants here and then go to Kansas to look for a wife. He's already been out there, on the bus, once. So, right now, he's living high, wide, and handsome, and he's not going to marry any of us Saltillo girls."

"Would you marry someone from Middlefield?" Branden asked.

"If he's a nice man, why not? If he's good to me and the kids, a good provider, then I'll have a good life. I want to be close enough that I can come home to visit. See all my little sisters and brothers. Families are important, and Middlefield isn't too far."

"You'd be happy with an arranged marriage?"

"I'd sure expect to get to know him first. But everybody wants to be happy. Raise a good family. As far as that goes, it means I'd have to stay Amish. Marry a good Amish man. And I've seen enough of the English world to know that they aren't happy. All the modern things they have, and they are not happy. Not very many are, anyways. And that isn't anything that drugs, sex, or alcohol can fix. No.

"I've had a little fun, OK? That's that. I don't need to see any more of the world. I'm going to take that drive up to Middlefield. Get serious about having a life. I'd made that decision even before Johnny got killed. That's why I told the bishop I wanted to be the first to talk today. I've had enough running wild for a lifetime. I don't need a cell phone, parties, anything like that. Not anymore. I'm going home to tell my parents I'll go to Middlefield. I've got relatives there, and I can stay a while. Meet someone nice. Get to know him. Make a life."

*   *   *

Henry Erb came into Interview A and sat glumly in the single chair at the end of the table. He slumped somewhat in the chair, trying for a casual pose, but his gaze darted about the room, and he fidgeted nervously with his fingers in his lap.

Branden said, "Interview with the sheriff didn't go so well, Henry?"

Erb shook his head stubbornly. "I'm not going to talk about drugs. I don't have to say anything."

Niell said, "We're not interested in drugs," and moved his chair down to Erb's end of the table.

Henry sat up, a weary curiosity showing in his expression.

Branden indicated Niell's move and asked, "May I?"

Erb raised his palms agreeably and said, "If it suits you."

Branden moved his chair to Erb's end of the table, and sat opposite Niell. "Henry," he said, "we're worried about Sara Yoder."

"I don't know where she is."

"You may know who took her," Niell said mildly.

Erb raised his brows and said, "I'm not thinking anyone actually took her."

Branden waited a beat, studying Erb's expression, and said, "The younger Yoder kids said some English strangers forced her into a car."

"I wouldn't be thinking they were strangers to Sara," Erb said.

Branden glanced at Niell, and frowned.

Tentatively, Erb asked, "It was Sara who told you about John Schlabaugh?"

"She showed us the barn," Branden said. "I'm not sure she knew his body was buried there when she called Cal."

"And she told you about drugs?"

"She said John Schlabaugh and Abe Yoder made a big drug deal with some Columbus outfit."

Erb drummed his fingers lightly on the table and said, "Are you sure you can trust what she told you?"

Branden pushed his chair back slightly from the table, putting some distance between him and Erb, and asked, "Is there a reason she'd tell us something wrong?"

Erb shrugged and smiled wanly, suggesting he knew more. "She's in love with one of the boys," he said forlornly, eyes fixed on the professor. "Not with the right one."

Branden held his stare. "Jeremiah Miller?" he asked.

"I'm not saying yes, and I'm not saying no. I'm just saying that John and Abe weren't the only ones involved in a drug deal."

Niell asked, "Do you think Sara would lie to protect Jeremiah?"

Erb tipped his head sideways, saying, "I'm not thinking that Sara is someone I can trust. That you can trust, I mean."

"What do you mean?" Branden asked.

"I'm just saying that maybe the people who came for Sara weren't strangers to her."

"Are you saying that Sara is dealing drugs herself?" Niell asked.

"I'm not going to talk about any drugs," Erb said, slumping again in his chair. "I really can't tell you anything more."

* * *

Andy Stutzman tripped on his own feet when he came into the room and fell forward, catching himself on the top of the metal table and dropping into the chair beside Professor Branden. Ellie poked her head through the doorway and said, "Andy Stutzman," by way of introduction.

Stutzman wiped his long blue sleeve across his lips, and slurred out, "Johnny Schlabaugh wasn't a bad person. They shouldn't talk about him that way."

Branden and Niell exchanged glances.

Andy sat glumly in his chair and focused his eyes, with difficulty, on the thin edge of the metal table. He gripped the armrests of his chair as if he needed a prop to sit up straight. He was a small man, with long black hair pulled into a ponytail at the base of his neck. He had sideburns as long as muttonchops, but no wider than a nail, and he was growing the ghost of a mustache, though evidently not having much success at it. He stank of beer.

Branden leaned forward and touched Stutzman's forearm lightly. Stutzman jerked his arm away.

Branden said, "Are you going to be OK, Andy?"

Stutzman craned his gaze around to find Branden and said, "I'm doing fine, just fine."

Branden smiled and looked at Ricky, shaking his head furtively. Niell gave a nod and said, "Maybe we should do this later, Mr. Stutzman."

Andy shouted, "Do it now!" and then said, more quietly, "I'm good to go. Got no trouble at all."

Branden asked, "Can you think where Sara Yoder might be?"

"Naw."

Niell said, "Can you tell us who she might have gone off with?"

Nothing from Stutzman but a blank, unfocused stare into middle space.

Branden said, "You do know that John Schlabaugh has been murdered?"

Stutzman groaned, "Why does everybody keep reminding me of that?"

"What's wrong, Andy?" Branden said.

"Wrong? Nothin's wrong. Just, is all, you know. The best guy in the world, Johnny Schlabaugh."

"You liked him a lot," Niell said. "Why not help us find who killed him?"

"Loved him! Best friend in the world. Johnny knew how to live! Knew fun, Johnny Schlabaugh. Best guy in the world."

Branden got Niell's attention and gave a sad shake of his head.

"OK, Andy," Niell said. "That's going to be all for today."

* * *

The other two boys, Ben Troyer and John Miller, each took their walks down to Interview B and then Interview A, and after an hour, the men and Ellie had finished talking with all of them. Robertson parked Niell and Branden in his office and walked Ellie down to her counter. Bishop Raber was still there, but all the kids had left. Robertson smiled and said, "I appreciate your help, Bishop."

Raber nodded wordlessly, and turned to leave. Reconsidering, he turned back to Robertson and said, "Did they tell you anything that will be useful in finding Sara Yoder?"

Robertson said, "If they did, it will have been in the second interview with Sergeant Niell and the professor. That's what we're going to talk about now."

"If they need to tell you more?" Raber asked.

"I'll get in touch with you. How can I reach you?"

"Cal Troyer is going to stay with us for a few days. You can call his cell phone."

With Niell and Branden back in his office, Robertson said, "I got nothing. What'd you two get?"

"We can forget Andy Stutzman for now," Branden said.

Robertson nodded. "Clearly."

"We got a weird something from Henry Erb," Ricky said.

Robertson waited.

Niell said, "Henry Erb suggested that Sara and Jeremiah were more involved in the drug business than Sara Yoder indicated to the professor."

"He's in love with her, too," Branden said. "I don't know how much we can trust him."

"What else did you get?" Robertson asked. "From the other kids."

Ricky took a straight-backed chair in front of Robertson's desk and said, "They all knew that John Schlabaugh and Abe Yoder had set themselves up to sell cheap drugs. Some of them were afraid, getting out of the mix while they could. Going back home, so to speak."

"Others weren't?" Robertson asked.

"There were a couple of cool ones," Branden said. "They sat in the chair at the far end of the table. Didn't really open up. But, we did get that John and Abe made a big buy from an outfit down by Columbus. And Henry Erb said that Sara and Jeremiah Miller had some of that action, too. Or words to that effect."

"You notice who was absent, Mike?" Robertson said.

"Jeremiah Miller."

"Don't you think that means something?"

Branden nodded pensively. "I'll go out to see him," he said. "Bring him back so you can have a talk with him."

"You've kept in touch with the Millers?"

"Caroline and I go out there for dinner once or twice a year. Jeremiah has always been shy around us."

"Is his granddaddy still the bishop?" Robertson asked.

"No," Branden said. "He died a few months back. Cal says Jeremiah wants to marry Sara Yoder."

Robertson said, "Then I'd expect him to be more forthcoming. Unless this Erb is right, and Jeremiah and Sara are part of the whole deal."

Ellie came in and said, "Here's that tape, Sheriff." She slid it into a video deck on the shelves behind Robertson's desk and punched Play.

On the screen, there was a long zoom shot across a parking lot with cars and pickup trucks. It was late afternoon or early evening, judging by the shadows. Over beside a brick wall, John Schlabaugh talked with a big redheaded man in jeans and a black leather vest. There was only faint audio, the rapid breathing of the person shooting the video. The man handed Schlabaugh a leather briefcase, looked around briefly at the parked cars, and turned and walked around the corner of the building. The video camera shook and then shut off as a soft voice whispered something celebratory in Dutch dialect.

Ellie switched the player off, and Branden said, "That's the briefcase we found at the cabin with Abe Yoder."

"I didn't see any money change hands," Ricky said.

"Maybe they'd paid for the drugs earlier," Branden said.

"More likely, they took the drugs on credit," Robertson said. "Dealers work it that way to get their hooks into you."

"Would those kids be that naive?" Ricky asked rhetorically.

"And who shot the video?" Robertson asked.

"I'm guessing it was Abe Yoder," Branden said.

"If you take this Erb seriously," Robertson said, "it could equally have been Sara or Jeremiah."

Ellie said, "Stan Armbruster called with the location of those GPS coordinates from Yoder's cell phone."

"Where's he at?" Robertson asked.

"Says he's at a country bar in Gahanna, east of Columbus. I took the radio call about ten minutes ago. He's waiting there now."

"Come on," Robertson said, and marched out to her radio consoles, the others following.

Ellie keyed her microphone and got Armbruster.

Robertson said, "Can you describe the building, Stan?"

"One-story, yellow brick building with a large gravel parking lot. It's a bar a little north of Gahanna, on U.S. Route 62."

"That matches our video," Branden said.

Robertson said, "Pull out, Stan. I don't want a cruiser sitting there very long."

"Leaving now," Armbruster reported.

Back in the sheriff's office, Branden said, "The DEA people will have it under surveillance if it's a hot spot."

Niell said, "Seems like we're counting on the DEA for a lot."

"We're doing everything we can do to find Sara," Robertson said. "I just like the idea that DEA might turn her up at one of their drug locations in Columbus. At the very least, I can't discount the possibility."

Branden nodded, thinking.

Ellie punched the intercom button and said, obviously shaken, "Bruce, Spits Wallace is dead."

14

Friday, July 23
5:30 P.M.

ARMS flung over his head, Spits Wallace lay on his back, bloody from wounds on his knee, abdomen, chest, and shoulder. His shotgun had dropped to the ground beside him. Nine-millimeter brass shell casings were strewn about on the driveway some eight or ten paces back. A neighbor, Bill Edger, scratched at his scruffy gray beard and said to Robertson, "It was a rapid tat, tat, tat kind of shooting. What I always thought a machine gun would sound like."

Robertson knelt in the gravel, hooked up a brass shell casing on the point of his gold pen, and studied it closely. "It's got a deep ejector mark," he said to Niell, and dropped it into a small plastic bag that Niell held open. "That's an automatic weapon, all right."

Back down the long gravel driveway, where five cruisers and Robertson's blue sedan were parked, deputies were walking the ground, eyes down, looking for evidence. A footprint in the driveway mud, in among the shell casings, had been marked for a plaster impression. The same prints walked up to Wallace, then proceeded to the kitchen door at the back of the house. Professor Branden was talking to Dan Wilsher at the back screen door, describing what he remembered about the booby traps inside the house.

"You have to know how to deactivate them," Branden said and reached into the doorway. "His daddy showed me all this when I was home one summer from college."

At head height, he felt for a string hooked to an eyelet. He pulled his hand back and said, "The first one is clear. We're OK in the kitchen."

Wilsher cleared men from around the door and slowly pushed the screen door open with an old hoe handle. Then he held the screen door back and pushed slowly with the hoe handle to open the inner door. Nothing happened, and the men with Wilsher relaxed noticeably.

Branden went into the kitchen, studied the room, and said, "We're all clear this far."

Wilsher went in next. Branden said, "Stay away from the doorway," and pointed to the entrance to the living room.

The two men searched the kitchen briefly. A fresh pot of coffee stood on the white metal kitchen counter. A half-eaten meal of fried chicken was left on the metal kitchen table. Muddy footprints marked the kitchen floor and led into the living room. Branden pointed out hooks on the far wall and said, "No shotgun on the hooks. Like I said, he didn't have the kitchen door rigged."

At the doorway into the living room, Branden knelt on the red linoleum and said, "Pressure plate here."

He eased the blade of his knife into a seam that defined a rectangle of loose tile, and pried the piece gently away from the floor. "If you step on this, you're gone," he said up to Wilsher.

With the linoleum tile removed, Branden studied the mechanism of a battery-powered switch. "This is bad," he said.

Carefully, so as not to disturb the electrical contacts on the switch, Branden pried one battery loose, and then the other. He slipped both batteries into his pocket, and stood up next to the doorway. "Have you got a mirror?" he asked Wilsher.

The lieutenant went to the kitchen door and called a deputy over. "There's a hand mirror in my trunk," he said. "In the toolbox."

The deputy nodded, trotted off, and returned shortly with a round mirror with a shiny metal back.

Wilsher delivered the mirror to the professor, and Branden held it to give a view around the doorway, at about head level. He groaned and then gave the mirror to Wilsher.

Wilsher had a look, stepped back, and whistled. "That's a real problem," he said.

"As far as I know, the only way to set it off," Branden said, "is the electronic switch."

"Provided Spits Wallace hasn't made any improvements since his dad put this in," Wilsher said.

Robertson appeared at the screen door to the kitchen and asked, "Any progress?"

Wilsher said, "We've got a double-barreled shotgun mounted on the other side of this wall. It's supposed to be on an electronic switch, and we've got the batteries out of that."

Branden said, "Trouble is, Spits Wallace could have a second trip mechanism."

Robertson said, "Spits Wallace wasn't that smart."

"Then you can lead us through this door," Branden said sarcastically.

Robertson said, "What's our best play, then?"

"Bring me a vest and a helmet," Branden said.

Robertson nodded and disappeared from in front of the screen door.

When the sheriff came back with the equipment, Branden suited up, dropped the faceplate on the helmet into position, lay flat on his back on the kitchen floor, and inched his way backward through the doorway, into the living room. He got his head through the doorway, looked up, and said, "There's a shotgun mounted along the wall, but there's no wire to the trigger."

Upright again in the kitchen, he added, "It can't be active. There are muddy footprints on the living room carpet. Someone has been in there. I'm betting the trap isn't active."

Wilsher said, "It's your call, Professor."

Branden frowned, lifted the faceplate on his helmet, and wiped sweat off his face with a paper towel from the kitchen counter. "I'll want to lift the muzzle off the peg, anyway, and step under it."

"How about if I reach around and push the muzzle up, while you scoot in on your back? You'll be out of range of the gun," Wilsher said.

"You're positive on that, are you, Dan?" Branden scoffed.

Wilsher shrugged.

From the screened door, Robertson said, "You do it, Dan. Crawl in under the muzzle, and take the shotgun off the wall."

"I know the mechanism," Branden said. "I'll do it."

"No," Robertson said through the screen. "It's going to be just like you said. No wire, no blast. Give Dan the vest and helmet, Mike."

Branden slipped out of the vest and helmet and helped Wilsher suit up and adjust the vest to his wider girth.

On his stomach, Wilsher slid into the living room, crouched against the wall under the shotgun, and gently lifted the weapon off its wall pegs. He cracked the chambers open and said, relieved, "Not loaded."

Branden stepped into the living room and Wilsher said, "It'd take your head off."

Branden smiled nervously.

Wilsher asked, "There's another one?"

"In the bedroom. Even if the first two traps weren't set," Branden said, "the third trap still might be loaded. There used to be only three. The last one's a spring-up switch plate weighted down with sacks of gold coins. If you move the coins, a shotgun rigged in the basement shoots you through the floor."

In the bedroom, they found the spring plate sprung up from the floor, no bags of gold coins weighing it down. In the basement, there was no shotgun mounted to shoot up through a hole in the ceiling. Branden climbed the steps back to the first floor and called "All clear" through the back screened door.

The search of the Spits Wallace property inside and out revealed nothing beyond the murder scene they had discovered when they had first come up the driveway. Robertson sent Wilsher out to release the deputy teams as the search wound down, and Niell, Robertson, and Branden stood in the kitchen to talk.

"There's no gold," Robertson said.

"No live booby traps," Branden said.

Wilsher came back into the kitchen and said, "One of my men took a radio call from Ellie. There's a DEA agent who was going to brief us at six o'clock."

"It's about time," Branden said. "Sara's been gone almost nine hours now."

Robertson walked out to the body, which had been maneuvered partway into a black body bag. The other men joined him. Missy Taggert was zipping him up.

"Let's have another look, Missy," Robertson said.

Missy unzipped the body bag, and the men crowded around. Spits Wallace was in the same dirty clothes he had been wearing that morning when Robertson and Branden had talked to him. Wallace's knees were caked with dried mud. His hands were black with coal, his nails chipped and stained yellow. A plug of tobacco was pushed out onto his beard by a protruding tongue. In his eyes, there was the startled look of a man who had been surprised by his own mortality.

15

Friday, July 23
6:50 P.M.

AGENT Tony Arnetto of the Drug Enforcement Administration stood with his back to the north-facing windows in Bruce Robertson's office at the jail and struggled vainly to bring a measure of calm back into his voice after the shouting match with Robertson had played to a draw. He was short, wiry, and dressed in a thousand-dollar suit more appropriate for the halls of Washington, D.C., than for the hills of east-central Ohio. The big sheriff's belligerence had brought his blood to a boil in record time.

His intransigence marked by the set of his jaw, Robertson stood behind his desk, as angry with Arnetto as he had ever been with anyone. Branden sat between them, in a chair in front of the sheriff's desk, surprised, despite long experience, by how quickly Robertson had been able to provoke the DEA agent into an outburst.

After a labored breath to calm himself, Arnetto said, "We can't take them down now. There's the bar, the house in Gahanna, and a score of dealers out on the street in Columbus alone. We're just not ready."

"You'll never be as ready as you want to be," Robertson argued, still heated.

"Look," Arnetto said, "it's complicated."

Pounding his desk, Robertson said, "It's not complicated! More likely than not, Sara Yoder is down there. She's sure not in Holmes

County anymore, or we'd have turned something up. We're going after her. You can take these drug clowns down at the same time."

Frustrated, Arnetto snapped his hand through the air and said, "You're not going to flush seven months of undercover work down the toilet on the off chance that she'll be in that bar. I keep telling you, we haven't seen her!"

Robertson kicked back against his chair and knocked it into the bookshelves behind his desk. He scratched furiously at his stiff burr haircut and scowled into the middle distance. He pulled the chair back to rights and sat down heavily. Ellie Troyer-Niell came into the office and stood tapping a steno pad with her pen, her face passive. Robertson gave her a glance, calmed himself on her account, and said, less aggressively, "Then send your man back into the Gahanna house. Find out if she's there."

"It's too soon," Arnetto said, responding in a measured way to Robertson's moderated tone. "Look, there's the bar on 62. You know about that from your videotape. Then there's the house in Gahanna. I shouldn't have told you about it, but there you are. If we take one or both of those places, we're going to lose all the Holmes County people this guy is running. That's five midlevel pushers and a dozen retailers out on your streets. We're just not ready to move."

Branden turned in his chair to face Arnetto more squarely, and said, "It is likely going to be this redhead's crew who took Sara away, Agent Arnetto. It's more than likely that this same crew is tied into John Schlabaugh's murder. Maybe Spits Wallace's, too."

"Who?" Arnetto asked.

"William Wallace," Branden said evenly. "He was killed today with a machine gun. He had told us earlier that some city boys had made a run at his place a while back."

"Made a run for what?" Arnetto asked, impatiently.

"Gold coins," Robertson said. "Look, it doesn't matter what it was for. We know where the bar is."

Arnetto shook his head and slapped his palms against his thighs in frustration. He moved to a chair beside Branden and sat down.

Ellie Troyer-Niell turned slowly and left quietly. Robertson planted his palms on his desk, trying to project less aggression.

Arnetto scratched a sideburn and said, "His name is Samuel White. Samuel 'Red Dog' White. He cooks Ecstasy for a three-state enterprise, and every time we raid his lab, he sets up somewhere else. We've never caught him dirty. He's too smart for that. And he's got his lab up and running again, God knows where, and if we go in looking for Sara Yoder, he'll spook, and that'll be seven months of undercover work shot to pieces, and we're just not going to do that, OK?"

Arnetto had managed to control his tone, but his face and neck were flushed with the effort. He shifted unhappily in his chair and rubbed at a pain in the side of his neck. He looked from Robertson to Branden and back at Robertson before saying, "I'm sorry. We're going to need at least three days to set up, before we let our guy go back to the Gahanna house. On what pretext, I don't know. But, even then, he's not going to be able to search the house for Sara Yoder. We could spoil the whole setup and still not find out if she's there."

Robertson nodded appeasingly, thought for a moment, and said, "Then you've got to take them all down. You can coordinate with us in Holmes County. Take them all down, Tony. It's the right thing to do, for Sara Yoder's sake."

Arnetto rubbed again at the throbbing pain in his neck, and shook his head. "It'd take at least three days to set it up, and we'd still not get all the Holmes County people."

Robertson said, "We don't have three days."

"You don't know that," Arnetto complained.

"We can't risk any delay," Robertson countered.

Arnetto hoisted his eyebrows in vexation, acknowledged the problem with a wave of his hand, and said, "I'll see what I can do."

Ellie came back through the door with her pen and steno pad, a blank expression on her face. She briefly caught Robertson's eye.

Branden stood and said, "I should be going."

Robertson said, "Hang back, Mike." Turning to his dispatcher, he said, "Ellie, please set Agent Arnetto up with all of our contact information."

Arnetto stood. "It'll be Monday, anyway, before we have something worked out."

"We'll be ready, Tony," Robertson said. "We'll do whatever we have to do, on this end. We'll cover Holmes County for you."

Arnetto jerked an unhappy nod and left with Ellie.

Branden sat back down and groaned, "That's not going to be soon enough."

Robertson said, "We're not going to wait."

"What do you mean?"

"We can't wait, Mike. Somebody has had her for nearly ten hours now, and I'm not gonna wait until Monday for those DEA pukes to put their ducks in a row."

"You've got a plan?"

"I'm gonna put someone in that bar tomorrow afternoon. We need to know who we're dealing with."

"All we have is the videotape," Branden observed.

"It's going to have to be enough."

"You can't raid the place."

"I had something softer in mind. Putting someone in there with a microphone clipped to his chest."

"Who have you got who doesn't look like a cop?"

"I figure on going in myself."

"You'll stand out like a sore thumb," Branden said, laughing.

"You got a better idea?"

"Dan Wilsher. He at least parts his hair."

"I don't know. Maybe Bobby Newell?"

"I'd be a better choice," Branden said.

Robertson held his eyes on the professor, measuring something, he wasn't sure what. Either his own harsh need or the professor's extravagant inner workings. He moved some papers around on his desk, rubbed at his scalp and said, eventually, "You do actually look scruffy enough to be a bar bum."

"Thanks ever so much, Sheriff," Branden drawled.

"You'd be in there a good hour, maybe more, if we do it right."

"Wired?"

"So you could talk to us, tell us what you see. But you wouldn't have ears."

"So, I'd sit, walk around, what?"

"We're going to want to know who's there. Who typically goes there. What kind of clientele they have. What's in the back rooms, if there are any. If Samuel White shows up, we'll hang a tail on him."

"This'll be risky," Branden said.

"If they're holding Sara Yoder there, it'll be worth it," Robertson said. "It'll be worth it even if all we get is a line on White. All we're going to do is sit down the road a ways and listen to what you tell us. All you're going to do is walk in, have a look around, sit a spell with a drink, and tell us what you see."

"All right," Branden said. "In the meantime, I'm going over to the hospital to visit Abe Yoder."

* * *

At Abe Yoder's bedside, Branden sat in a visitor's chair and listened to the IV motor click its medicine into the vein on the back of Yoder's pale hand. A plump Amish lady who had introduced herself as Orpha Buckholder sat in a corner chair, with knitting in her lap. She wore a dark green dress, white bodice, gray hose, soft black shoes, and a white prayer cap.

Abe Yoder mumbled an occasional unintelligible phrase, and intermittently pleaded, "Nicht Schiezzen." At one point, he roused and asked for a drink of water, and Orpha Buckholder got up and put a small ice cube in his mouth.

Branden said, "You've done this before," remembering his own desperate ordeal in the hospital one summer, after a murderer had crushed his leg in a struggle for a gun.

Orpha said, "The ice is better for them. It just melts, and they don't have to work a straw."

Branden nodded grimly and got out of his chair. He stretched his arms over his head, and went out into the hall to stretch his legs. Taking the elevator to the cafeteria, he bought a can of Diet Pepsi and went back to the room. Orpha Buckholder was standing in the hall, and two nurses were working on the bed sheets in Abe Yoder's room.

"He's been throwing up," Orpha said, "and he's awake."

Branden slipped into the room, stood at the foot of the bed, and waited for the nurses to finish cleaning up Yoder. They managed to get a clean sheet under him, and a clean blanket over him, and then they called on the intercom for housekeeping services. As they left, Branden moved to Yoder's side and pushed gently on his shoulder. Yoder opened his eyes and quizzed the professor with his expression.

"I'm Mike Branden, Abe. I found you in the cabin."

Yoder squeezed his eyes closed and moved his head slowly from side to side. He appeared to drift off, and he dozed for several minutes, then he opened his eyes wide, as if he had clawed himself out of a hideous nightmare. Weakly he said, in a voice almost too soft to hear, "What's another word for red, Mr. Branden?"

Unsure that he had heard correctly, Branden said, "Red?"

With effort, Yoder whispered, "What's another English word for red?"

"Pink?" Branden asked.

Yoder moved his head very slowly to indicate no.

"Rose?"

No answer.

Branden laid his hand on Yoder's head, and Yoder opened his eyes. "Crimson," Branden said.

Yoder mouthed the word and then said it out loud.

Branden gave his shoulder a gentle shake, and Yoder said, "Crimson mist."

Branden leaned in close and said, "Abe, stay with me. What is crimson mist?"

Yoder swallowed hard and said, "Big black revolver."

"Yes."

"Bucked like a horse."

"Big revolver? When?"

"Crimson mist. Blew out the side of Johnny's head."

"What are you saying, Abe?"

"That's what I saw when the bullet went through Johnny's head."

16

Friday, July 23
8:45 P.M.

THE tall silver maples on the front lawn at the Miller residence were filled with the raucous birdsong of starlings as Professor Branden pulled his truck to a stop on the gravel lane beside the Millers' white picket fence. Several children who had been playing on the front lawn stood quietly and watched him walk down to the driveway and turn in. With a mixture of extreme shyness and advanced curiosity, they slowly matched his progress toward the house, and then stood in a cluster as he mounted the steps.

The youngest of the children was about two, still in diapers. There were two beautiful girls of four or five, in rose dresses of heavy fabric, bare feet poking out from under the folds. Three boys five to eight years old wore matching blue shirts with oval necks and string ties, black suspenders, and blue denim trousers. They, too, were barefoot. When Branden knocked on the screen door, the children crowded up to the porch and peered through the railing slats, the oldest boy balancing the youngest child on his hip.

The lady who came to the door was known to Branden as Isaac Miller's wife, Annie. She knew Branden from the visits he and Caroline had made to see her mother-in-law, Gertie Miller. Gertie was mother to Isaac and seven other boys, among them Jonah Miller, aka Jon Mills, who had died one summer before Branden and Cal Troyer could figure out a way to help him. Jonah was the father of the errant Jeremiah Miller, the reason for Branden's visit this Friday evening.

Annie nodded politely, held the screen door open, and let Branden into the two-story white frame house.

Branden said, "I won't stay long, Annie. I just thought I'd visit a while with Gertie."

"She's around back," Annie said, and motioned for Branden to pass through the house. Instead, he backed out past the screened door and said, "I'll just go around the side."

As he descended the porch steps, Branden playfully said, "Hi, kids," to the children. He got a smile or two from the younger ones, and expressions of reserved amusement from the older ones. They all followed silently, stepping around to the side of the house, and down the driveway to the back.

Behind the big house, there was a small daadihaus that Isaac Miller had helped his father build the summer that Branden had worked their case. Branden remembered the concrete footers that the men had been pouring the day he had come out to confront Eli Miller, the bishop, about his son Jonah. The daadihaus had stood on those footers behind the big house since then, and served as a dwelling for Eli and Gertie Miller after Eli had retired from farming. Isaac's older brothers had families, now, and they were farming land that had been subdivided to the boys. Isaac was now raising his own family in the big house, and the little band of curious Amish children that followed Branden now would be Isaac's and Annie's children, Gertie's grandchildren. First cousins to Jeremiah.

At the back of the house, Annie Miller appeared, holding a dish-towel, and spoke a few words of Dutch. The children, obviously disappointed, filed back around to the front of the house without verbal protest.

Branden found Gertie Miller in a rocking chair on the small wooden porch of the daadihaus. The porch and the walkway to the big house were covered over with a grape arbor. Gertie saw Branden coming down the walkway and tried to get out of her chair, but Branden said, "Please, Gertie, don't get up."

Gertie Miller sat with her twisted fingers nestled awkwardly in her lap. On each wrist, she wore a copper bracelet for the pain of the arthritis that had crippled her. Purple and lavender yarn and two long, green knitting needles lay on the floorboards beside her rocker. She reached over the arm of her chair and slowly raised the work for Branden to see. Unable to grasp the needles properly, she had to scoop the whole yarn affair up in a bundle to display it. With an icy humor, she smiled and said, "I can't work the needles, anymore, Professor. They'll put an old goat like me out to graze."

Branden smiled affectionately, gently took the work from her fingers, and said, "It's your turn to rest, Gertie."

She croaked out a "Ha!" and said, "Grannies like me have the rest of their lives to rest. Today, I'd settle for a bucket of potatoes to peel. Maybe some laundry to hang. Old goats have to keep busy to earn their keep."

Branden pulled a Shaker chair up beside her and said, "I was sorry to hear that Eli died, Gertie."

"Three months, now," she observed. "Eli went out hard. He had pneumonia. He couldn't breathe."

"I'm sorry, Gertie," Branden said. He laid the knitting in his lap.

Gertie's eyes seemed to take an inward focus, and she sat quietly for a spell. Branden sat beside her and waited. Old sorrows played in the muscles around her eyes, as she drifted among her memories.

She was dressed in a high-necked, pleated dress of porpoise gray that flowed down to her black leather shoes. Her white hair was tied up in a bun, and topped with a black bonnet and hood. Her eyelids were red, and her nostrils were moist, as if she suffered from summer allergies. At intervals she pulled a wrinkled hankie from a pocket on her white apron and awkwardly pushed it with her osseous fingers, first to her eyes and then to her nose. When her fingers were asked to put the hankie back in the apron pocket, they replied with a measure of stiff pain. She sighed reflexively, and settled lower in her chair. "Eli was a good man," she said. "He died hard."

Branden said, "He was a good bishop," and she nodded a firm concurrence.

"It almost killed him to lose Jonah, but he didn't let anyone see that," Gertie said.

Branden said, "I've seen Jeremiah from time to time."

Gertie looked up at him. "In town?" she asked.

"He drove his buggy up to our house a couple of times, the year before last. Just seemed to want to sit and talk about life."

"He's not usually the talkative type," Gertie said.

"I hear he wants to marry."

Gertie started rocking her chair. "One of the Yoder girls," she said. "Over to Salem church."

"I'm trying to find him, Gertie," Branden said.

"Don't tell his uncle Isaac," she said, "but he keeps a car up the way."

"Can you tell me where to look for him?" Branden asked.

"He's out with his buggy, Professor. Sometimes he's gone all night. It's Friday, so I expect he's gone courting."

"Do you know who his friends are, Gertie? Do they ever come around?"

"I don't see him that much," Gertie said. "We have our moments, every month or so. We'll sit and talk by ourselves. He saves me for that special need. He talks about the people who kidnapped him. And especially about the day you saved him up on the lake. But then he'll turn quiet. He draws himself inward, like a spider backing into a hole, and that's when he wants me to talk about his father. When he's had enough, he gets up slowly and goes. I know, then, that he won't need me for a spell."

"You're probably the only one he can talk to about these things," Branden said.

"Each time we've talked, I've had the impression I've saved him from something that's chasing him. Something dreadful. He has his father's blood to wander. He has his father's restless mind."

"I thought if I could find him, I might be able to help him with that."

"Has there been some trouble?"

"Yes, Gertie. A boy has been killed."

"Is Jeremiah involved?"

"I don't think so, but I need to find him."

"Has it got something to do with that Johnny Schlabaugh?"

"Yes. He's the one who's been killed."

"And young Abe Yoder?"

"He's been hurt, too."

"Jeremiah says he keeps his car in a barn, beside Johnny Schlabaugh's trailer. You could try looking there."

"I was out there, earlier."

"When Jeremiah is away from home this long, it always means he is out in his car."

Branden rose to his feet and said, "I'll let you know what I find."

"Tell him to come home, Professor."

"I will."

"Tell him to come home, and stay."

"I will try."

Gertie Miller struggled out of her chair to stand bent over in front of Branden. "He has a good future, here," she said.

She fumbled with her stiff fingers, withdrew her hankie from her apron pocket, and dried her eyes and nose. "His uncles have cut out a tract of land for him. If he marries and settles down, he'll have a good life. Like Eli and me. Tell him it's no good, Professor, chasing all around town. Remind him what happened to his father."

As he left, the professor took a call from Bruce Robertson. "Everything has changed, Mike," Robertson said. "Abe Yoder ran off from the hospital."

17

Friday, July 23
10:15 P.M.

"I DON'T like it, Michael," Caroline said. "Not one bit."

She was seated at her bureau, dressed for bed, brushing out her long, auburn hair. The professor was in bed, propped up on pillows, in his blue pajamas.

"Nobody knows me down there," he said. "It'll just be a quick 'in and out.'"

She got up from the bureau, stretched out beside him on the bed, and said, "You don't even know that this Red Dog White is the one who has her."

"It's just a guess. But a good one."

"You ought to let this Arnetto work out a plan to catch everyone all at once."

"It'll take too long. We may have to do it that way in the end. Wait for Arnetto, if we have to. But we can still try for Sara tomorrow. Work the one good lead we do have."

"What lead is that, Michael? A video of some unknown bar?"

"It's the right place. Arnetto confirmed it. You need to stop worrying."

"I need to wring Bruce Robertson's neck, is what I need to do."

Branden laughed softly and pulled her to him. "Cal's out at Bishop Raber's. If either Abe Yoder or Jeremiah Miller turns up, he'll know it right away. Then they might be able to give us a better lead to look for Sara."

"Do you really think Abe Yoder is going to wander back home now?"

"I was just saying."

"Are you going to carry a gun?"

"Ankle holster, probably."

"So you do actually think that it is dangerous."

"Country bars can be dangerous any day of the week. I'm just going to sit and have a drink."

Caroline pushed herself away from him, plumped her pillow against the headboard, and sat up. "Tell me again about this Red Dog," she said.

The professor told her everything he knew. The base house in Gahanna that Arnetto had described. The bar where John Schlabaugh had taken possession of a briefcase. The cabin where he had found Abe Yoder. The disappearance of Abe Yoder from the hospital. The apparent kidnapping of Sara Yoder at the Salem Cemetery. The grave site of John Schlabaugh. The cell phones with messages in code and GPS coordinates. The forlorn look in Sara Yoder's eyes when she had seen the body in the grave.

After he had fallen asleep, Caroline eased out of bed and sat at her bureau, brushing out her hair in the dark, her mind wandering the landscape of the case he had painted for her. He was right. It would be enough, at this point, simply to rescue Sara Yoder. But Abe Yoder was missing, too. And why hadn't Jeremiah Miller made it to the jail interviews that afternoon? Why would Abe Yoder hide away in an old cabin for the better part of a week, not seeking treatment for his wound? What did Spits Wallace have to do with any of this?

On the surface, it looked like a drug deal gone bad. Under the surface, there were too many questions. What did Abe Yoder hope now to accomplish? Was he simply running scared? Hiding from the people who had shot him? Or had he been involved in Schlabaugh's murder himself? Or had Jeremiah? Once partners and friends, then divided against each other over the money or the drugs? That seemed plausible. Then again, it didn't. Not for Amish.

Then, what of Sara? How much truth and how much evasion had there been in the few things she had told Cal Troyer and her husband? What had she really known when she had led them to the grave? Giving her the benefit of the doubt, even if Sara Yoder were brought back home safely, would she stay? Stay Amish after so great an ordeal? Or go English? Her choice, to make, if she could only be given the chance.

Or had her story been all an act? What they knew of her was, essentially, only what she had told them. And what had she told them?

That a gang of Amish kids was in way over their heads with a Rumschpringe gone bad. That there was a grave in a red barn in the country. That John Schlabaugh had been a drifter. The worst kind of drifter, if she were right. That John Schlabaugh and Abe Yoder had gotten them all in enough trouble to last a lifetime.

SATURDAY, JULY 24

18

PROFESSOR Branden drove up the Doughty Valley to the Schlabaugh trailer and found a buggy pushed back under the hickory
trees next to the barn. In a pasture behind the barn, a Standardbred horse munched on a tall mound of hay in a corner of the fence.
When Branden inspected the buggy, he found a bloody hospital
dressing on the floorboards, and bloodstains on the right side of
the seat. In the barn, the tractor and farm implements stood alone
in the center avenue. The two cars were gone.

Branden tried the door to the trailer and found it locked. He
climbed back into his truck and drove down County 19 to Township 110, then looped back into the valley where the Yoders and
Rabers lived. At Bishop Raber's brick house, he found Cal's truck
parked amid several buggies. Cal and the bishop were seated in lawn
chairs on the back porch with several solemn men, plates of bacon,
eggs, and corn bread in their laps. Cal motioned with his fork for
Branden to take a seat on a wooden chair next to him, and as Branden sat down, a lady in a long, green dress and flowered kitchen
apron came out onto the porch and asked the bishop if their visitor would be having breakfast too. Raber looked at Branden, and
Branden nodded and thanked her. She went back inside, letting the
screened door slap shut, returning with a heaping plate for the professor and a cup of coffee that she put on the porch boards beside
his chair. After he had taken several bites and drunk some coffee,

Branden said, "I think Jeremiah Miller picked Abe Yoder up at the hospital," and explained what he had discovered at John Schlabaugh's barn.

Raber asked, "Was there a lot of blood?"

Branden shrugged. "Enough. He's got to be hurting. I'm not surprised that Abe left the hospital. I'm not even surprised that Jeremiah helped him do it. Abe could have called Jeremiah, or Jeremiah could have just showed up. Nobody would notice two Amish kids in a buggy. If Jeremiah had taken his car, that would be different, so they obviously thought this through together. What I wonder, though, is where they have gone. What they plan to do."

Cal said, around a mouthful of corn bread, "Jeremiah will know that Sara was taken. Maybe they think they can do something about that."

"I'm surprised he can travel," Branden said. "Abe, I mean."

Raber asked, "Both cars were gone at John Schlabaugh's place?"

Branden nodded, ate a bite. "One was Jeremiah's, as I remember. Who owns the other one? Remind me."

"John Miller," Raber said. "He lives out by Gypsy Springs School, on the other side of Saltillo."

Branden laid his plate on the porch boards and took up his coffee. He stared at the cup a while, took a sip, and said, "Cal, I'd like to borrow your truck."

"Sure. Why?" Cal said.

"Bruce Robertson and I have a little something cooked up for later this afternoon, and it'd look better if I showed up in a carpenter's truck. Working man. That sort of thing."

Cal fished out his keys, saying, "You'll need to get some gas."

Branden traded keys and said, "If things work out, we may be able to locate Sara Yoder. It's a long shot, but it's worth the gamble."

Raber said, "I'm going to visit families this afternoon with the preachers. Is there anything you want us to do?"

With level conviction, Branden said, "Yes. I want you to pray."

19

Saturday, July 24
1:15 P.M.

BRANDEN pushed through the rusty bar door, dressed for the afternoon in a red work shirt with snap-down pockets and baggy black jeans. His leather belt sported the Smith & Wesson logo. He wore an old pair of work boots, and the cuffs of his jeans came down over both the boot tops and, on the left, a small ankle holster carrying a stainless AMT Backup pistol in the diminutive caliber .380.

Inside the door, on the left, a jukebox played a fast-paced country song, and on a small dance floor covered with sawdust, a middle-aged couple was doing a vigorous two-step.

Beyond the dance floor, further to the left, a row of wooden booths ended in a metal door marked Office. One young couple sat in the last booth, smoking cigarettes and drinking beer in the dim light.

Branden stepped back to the bar, got a draft beer, and took it to a front corner booth, to the right of the entrance, where he'd be out of the line of sight of anyone coming into the bar. As he sat down, he spoke quietly into his microphone, "Seven cars out front, five people in view, counting the bartender."

Three fans spaced evenly in the ceiling made slow, quiet turns in the air. The only windows were glass blocks set high in the walls, admitting a small fraction of the bright afternoon light. The wood floor was old and irregular. In the center of the bar there were rustic pine tables and chairs, all empty, and on Branden's right there was another row of booths lining the wall. The bar itself ran the length of the back wall, with a dozen empty barstools standing in front of it. It had a black Naugahyde bumper, and on the left stood several tall levers marked colorfully with the logos of the beers available on tap. Behind the bar, the liquor bottles were lined up on a long shelf in front of a wall-length mirror.

Robertson was down the road a mile or so, in a high school parking lot, listening in his blue sedan, receiver on the dash, an earplug in his ear. Behind the school, Ricky Niell was parked in a Holmes County cruiser with one other deputy.

While Branden waited, three older men came in and took a booth on the right, two down from Branden and closer to the bar. Two were in blue service uniforms, and the third wore jeans, a T-shirt, and a red ball cap. Red Cap went to the bar and spoke to the bartender, and then sat down with the other two men.

The jukebox switched to a country waltz, and the dancing couple sat down in one of the booths along the left wall. The bartender, a large, florid man in a white shirt, jeans, and black leather vest, came out to the booth with the three men. He leaned over the table, took some folding money from Red Cap, and slipped it into the left front pocket of his jeans, under his waist apron. Then he passed a small plastic bag from his right jeans pocket to the man. The three men sat for a minute and then left quietly.

Nursing his beer, Branden sat for half an hour and described the comings and goings inside the bar. Five people came in, transacted quietly with the bartender, and left without having a drink. The dancing couple fed quarters into the jukebox, took another turn with a two-step, and left after paying their tab.

The young couple on the left moved to the bar and sat to talk quietly with the bartender. He listened, leaning forward on the bar, then shook his head and stepped back. The young man waved him closer and put several bills on the bar, and the bartender scooped them up, seeming annoyed.

He went through the door marked Office and came out with a middle-aged man in a well-tailored gray suit. Gray Suit spoke with the young couple and went back into the office, having instructed the bartender to wait. When he came out, Gray Suit walked up to the young man on the barstool, pushed the folding money roughly into the boy's shirt pocket, shoved him off the stool, and ordered the boy and girl out of the bar. Before he went back through the office door, Gray Suit spoke angrily to the bartender, who backed up, slipped in behind the bar, and started washing out glasses in the sink under the bar. In the mirror behind the bar, Branden saw Abe Yoder and Jeremiah Miller coming through the front door, dressed English from head to toe.

Jeremiah was in blue Wranglers with no belt. The pocket of his light blue sport shirt held a pack of cigarettes. His black track shoes had the Nike swoosh. Abe Yoder was wearing black designer jeans with a wide leather belt. He had pulled up his pink-and-gray-striped, button-down shirt so that it hung loose on the left side. He was in white running shoes with elaborate, angled soles.

Jeremiah walked aggressively, straight back to the bar, stopping once to turn and measure Abe Yoder's progress behind him. Abe followed slowly, his left arm stiff against his side, favoring his left leg as he maneuvered between the tables.

Branden whispered into his microphone, "Abe Yoder and Jeremiah Miller just walked in," and held his hands, fingers locked, in front of his mouth, elbows propped on the table for cover.

When Yoder made it up to the bar, the bartender had already started arguing loudly with Jeremiah Miller. Yoder joined in the argument, and Branden heard the bartender shout, "Get out!"

When neither Yoder nor Miller gave any indication that they intended to leave, the bartender came out around the end of the bar, his face flushed with anger. Yoder backed up as the man advanced, and bumped his left hip against one of the barstools. He doubled over, holding his left side with both hands. The bartender, ignoring Yoder, took Jeremiah roughly by the arm and started marching him toward the door. Abe got a grip on an ashtray with his right hand and threw it hard against the mirror behind the bar, shattering it and a half dozen bottles on the liquor shelf.

Gray Suit pushed through the office door, took hold of Yoder's shirt collar, and threw a heavy punch into Yoder's ribs. Yoder folded to his knees and was hauled, gasping, to his feet. Then the bartender marched both Miller and Yoder out the door to the parking lot.

When the bartender came back through the door, Branden handed him a five and said, "Keep the change."

His back was to the bar, and he didn't see Gray Suit advancing on him as he handed over the bill. Gray Suit crooked his left arm around the professor's neck in a chokehold from the back and threw a vicious right-hand punch into Branden's side. Branden's knees gave way and he sagged into the chokehold. Another quick punch took Branden to his knees. He passed out briefly. When he came to, the man had him pinned face down on the floor, his arm cranked painfully up against his back, a kidney taking the full weight of his attacker's knee.

Gray Suit fumbled with Branden's ankle holster, pulled out the AMT Backup, and cracked it onto the back of Branden's skull, growling, "Nobody brings a gun into my bar!"

Gray Suit pitched the little silver pistol to the bartender, pulled Branden to his feet, and slammed him out through the metal door into the parking lot. The bartender came out, and Gray Suit barked, "Back inside, Jimmy!" and smashed the edge of his hand against the back of Branden's neck.

When the bartender was gone, Gray Suit said, "I saw you talking into your shirt, dummy. You the law?"

Branden said, "Figure it out for yourself."

Gray Suit spun Branden around and took him with both fists by the front of his shirt. A quarter inch off his nose, he whispered,

"That was for Jimmy's benefit. Tell Arnetto I still don't know where the X lab is. Tell him to find that lab before he does anything that'll blow my cover."

*　　*　　*

By the time Branden made it to the back of the parking lot, Jeremiah was helping Abe Yoder into his Chevy. He looked up, saw Branden, recognized him, and froze. Branden started forward, cradling the back of his neck, and Jeremiah ran around the front of his car, jumped behind the wheel, and sped off toward Gahanna.

Standing on the gravel parking lot, Branden reported, "Yoder is hurt—punched in the ribs. Miller is driving your way in a white Chevy Nova."

Branden hobbled to Cal's truck and eased himself into the driver's seat, wincing. He followed the Nova at a more sedate pace. A mile down the road, he saw that Ricky Niell's cruiser had forced Jeremiah's Chevy over onto the school parking lot. When Branden pulled up, Yoder was slumped down in the passenger seat of the Chevy. The sheriff's deputy was already leaning in through the open door, pressing a large gauze bandage to Abe Yoder's side. Branden limped up to Miller's car, saw the blood on the compress, and turned back to the cruiser.

Jeremiah Miller sat sideways in the backseat of Niell's cruiser, holding his head in his hands, feet out on the pavement. Ricky Niell, in the front passenger seat, was making a radio call for an ambulance.

Robertson stood beside his blue sedan with a radio microphone in his hand, making another call. When Branden came up to him, Gray Suit from the bar was rolling a red Lexus by the scene, eyeing the Holmes County cruiser with obvious agitation and talking on a cell phone.

Branden lifted his chin at the passing car to draw Robertson's attention to it without staring at Gray Suit, and said, "That guy's from the bar. Works in the office. He's DEA, from what I can tell.

Gave me a message for Arnetto. If he's smart about being under-cover, he's calling Samuel White. We're going to have to take Abe Yoder someplace where he can't be found. They still think he has their briefcase full of drugs."

Robertson read the license plate on the passing car and took out a small spiral notebook to write down the number.

"They sell more drugs in that bar than booze," Branden said, rubbing at the pressure in his temples. "It was a stupid play for Yoder to let himself be seen down here if he couldn't return the briefcase."

"This is Tony Arnetto's territory," Robertson said. "If we take Yoder to Mount Carmel East, I can get a face-to-face with Arnetto this afternoon."

Branden opened the back door of Robertson's car and flopped onto the seat on his back, feet sticking out.

Robertson said, "You gonna be all right, Mike?"

"In a minute."

"Why's your ankle holster hanging out loose?"

"That's thanks to Tony Arnetto's undercover man. He helped me dispose of the AMT in an unsafe manner."

20

Saturday, July 24
3:00 P.M.

"THE man in the gray suit is my guy!" Arnetto fumed indignantly. "He's my agent. What did you think you were doing?"

Robertson and Branden were seated in a small conference room on the second floor, above the emergency suites, at Mount Carmel East Hospital, in the eastern suburbs of Columbus. Arnetto sat with his back to the glass window of the conference room door, blocking entrance to anyone who might try to interrupt them. Branden met Arnetto's hostile gaze squarely. Robertson fought for control of his emotions.

With forced calm, Robertson said, "You're overreacting."

Branden glanced sideways at the smoldering sheriff, enjoying the full irony, despite the unpleasant circumstances, of Robertson's accusing anyone of that particular mistake. He laid his palms flat on the conference table, and said, "Sara Yoder deserves more than this. We were trying to help her."

"What if Samuel White had been there?" Arnetto complained, and sat down across from them at the table.

"He wasn't," Branden said. "And because I was there, we now have Yoder and Miller in custody."

"The man you saw in the gray suit is Robert French, from St. Louis. We brought him here as a fresh face to infiltrate White's operation. He had some believable credentials from St. Louis after a successful undercover stint there in the mob. They still think he's a right guy with them. So he won't blow both covers, he's telling Samuel White that those two Amish kids came into the bar this afternoon. He's telling White that Yoder was taken by ambulance to the hospital, and that a sheriff's cruiser was involved. Before we leave this room, White will have someone in the emergency room to check Yoder out. It won't matter that I've got agents down there with him. Someone will tell White where Yoder is. You can bet on that. Then, they're going to take him out."

"French doesn't have to tell White anything," Robertson said, knots of muscle jumping in the corner of his jaw.

"Yes he does!" Arnetto said. "If he doesn't, the bartender will. And I'm not ready to move on those arrests yet. I told you, it's got to be organized meticulously. French needs time to try to locate White's Ecstasy lab. We're sending in someone else from St. Louis with a bigger Ecstasy order than White normally handles. We think that'll flush out his labs for us."

Robertson argued, "You don't have to get the lab. Just take out White, the bar, the Gahanna house, everything you've got. If that doesn't turn up Sara Yoder, then we can interrogate White."

"You think White would turn her over to us? Admit to kidnapping on top of everything else?"

"He would if you made him a good enough deal."

"If you think I'm going to make any deals with White at this stage of the game, you're an idiot."

Ricky Niell pushed in through the glass conference room door, and escorted Jeremiah Miller behind Arnetto to a seat at the head of the table. He caught Robertson's eye, tipped his head at Jeremiah, and sat down between Arnetto and Miller.

Across the table, Robertson considered Niell's gesture and appeared to capitulate. To Arnetto, he said, "OK, Tony. I don't like it, but we'll do it your way."

Arnetto got out of his chair, puzzled by what had transpired. He looked long at Jeremiah, as if he were considering holding him on charges. To Robertson, he said, "Stay clear of this, Bruce. Give us until Monday."

Robertson signaled acquiescence with a wave of his hand. "Monday," he said, eyes focused on the flat of the table.

Arnetto left.

Robertson turned to Niell and said, "This had better be good."

Niell said, "We need to let Jeremiah talk with the professor."

Robertson said, glowering, "He can talk to me!"

Not in the least fazed by the sheriff's hostility, Ricky said, "Jeremiah has assured me that if he can talk to Mike for a while, he'll tell us everything he knows about Abe Yoder, John Schlabaugh, and Samuel White's briefcase full of drugs. What he didn't know before, he's learned from Abe Yoder today. You're going to want to hear what he has to say. But first, he wants to talk with the professor."

*　*　*

When Branden brought Robertson and Niell back into the conference room, Jeremiah had Branden's wadded handkerchief in his fist, dabbing tears from his red and swollen eyes. He straightened when the men came in, and he glanced to the professor for reassurance. Branden nodded compassionately and said to Robertson, "Jeremiah helped Abe Yoder leave the hospital. He's got some things to say. I've heard most of it, and I've reassured him that he's not in trouble with the law. That's what he really wanted to talk with me about, Bruce, before he talked with you."

When Niell and the sheriff were seated, Jeremiah began.

"I've been crazy in the head about Sara. I know the kind of people who took her. The younger Yoder boys who saw her taken say it was a big redheaded man. That's Samuel White, who Abe says shot Johnny Schlabaugh. He saw it, he said. I believe him.

"We thought, why not take the briefcase back to the bar? A lot of the drugs was still there. And the money, too. So I took a buggy to the hospital, and me and Abe went back to the cabin to get the briefcase. That's how we thought we'd get Sara back. Turn over the briefcase.

"But someone took it. So Abe and me, we tried to buy another gun from that shop over by Wilmot, but the guy wouldn't sell us one. So that's when I thought I'd trade them, her for me. Something like that. That's why we went to the bar. White still thinks we have his drugs. But the bartender there threw us out, and the professor saw us.

"Abe was hurt and bleeding again, so we just ran. I thought I'd get him to a hospital. That's when you stopped us by the school.

"I'm losing my mind, thinking about Sara. I can't think hardly straight anymore. But one thing I did remember, talking with Officer Niell, here. He asked me all those questions. Made me remember.

"One day, about two months ago, I followed Johnny Schlabaugh in my car. He met that big redhead at Becks Mills, and they drove back toward Charm and turned onto a weedy lane, into some trees. It was just an old barn there, so I didn't think anything of it. But now it's different. They've put in electric. It's way back in, nowhere from anywhere, and there's a big electric line going right in there."

Robertson asked, "Can you show us where that is?"

Jeremiah said, "I can take you there, or you can go yourself. I wrote down the GPS coordinates. You're gonna want them, because White called me on Johnny's secret phone."

"Wait a minute," Robertson said. "Why do you have Schlabaugh's cell phone?"

"Abe took it when he buried Johnny. Thought it'd be safer to use. There's no way of tracing that kind of prepaid phone, he said."

Branden asked, "Then how did you get it?"

"I've been helping Abe out at the cabin where you found him. He gave it to me three days ago. It was me who ran off when you showed up at the cabin."

21

CAL TROYER took the professor's call as the last glimmer of twilight was fading from the valley at Salem Cemetery. The professor was with the sheriff's men. There would be a rescue attempt that night.

Cal listened intently and spoke briefly, then switched off as the purple martins darted overhead, making their last sorties for mosquitoes in front of the Albert P. Yoder residence. The cricket song in the pastures was strident, the low, murmuring notes of cattle mixed in. The yellow flicker of lantern light shined from several windows in the big house. Cal stood on the lawn between the house and barn and sought out the stars overhead. Spoke a prayer for the night.

Some of the news was good, he mused. The young Miller boy was safe, although his role in the troubles was unclear. Abe Yoder, though wounded, was at least in good hands at Mt. Carmel East. But Sara Yoder had not been found. Most troubling was the story of Samuel Red Dog White, who now held Sara's fate in his hands. No, Cal corrected himself, White held only her life in his hands. Her fate was in the hands of God.

Eyes lifted to the heavens, Cal listed for himself the tidings he would bear. The prayers he would organize with Bishop Raber, and the vigils they would keep, as Branden and Robertson searched desperately for Sara. As the hours passed by. Before Tony Arnetto could organize his people in Columbus.

First, to Miriam and Albert P. Yoder: Abe is safe for now. His stitches have torn open. Infection has taken hold once again. His fever is a danger to him as much as the wound. Pray for healing.

To Gertie Miller in the Doughty Valley: Jeremiah is unharmed. He is in the custody of the sheriff, as much for his safety as for his duplicity in any crime. Pray for continued safety.

To Albert O. Yoder and his wife Martha: Sara is still missing. Her life has been threatened by men unworthy even to speak her name. Pray for her rescue.

To Bishop Irvin Raber: All is not lost. Call your people together. Your leadership and righteousness are needed, now more than ever. Call the people to minister to one another in spirit. To pray for courage, as Sara Yoder's life is held in the balance. In the hands of English men, friend and foe.

And pray, most of all, for God's hand to work in all of this. For, when have the *Gemie*, the people, ever been able to do anything more powerful than pray? When has faith mattered more? Faith that God's mercy covers John Schlabaugh. Covers equally his family, floundering in grief. Covers the union of the body of believers. Covers the necessities of the next telling hours.

SUNDAY, JULY 25

22

Sunday, July 25
12:58 A.M.

BRANDEN and Robertson stole down the lane under cover of trees in the dark, and came within sight of a dilapidated, one-story barn lit by a halogen floodlamp mounted on the front corner. At the far limit of the broad light cast by the security flood, there stood a short, single-wide trailer on concrete blocks. Facing the barn, a small window of the trailer glowed with a faint yellow light shadowed once, then twice, by a figure moving inside. Robertson shielded Jeremiah Miller's GPS receiver by cupping his hand over the display, and checked the coordinates. He turned to Branden and nodded. Then he pointed to the trailer's window and whispered, "At least one in the trailer."

As he spoke, a man in dungarees and a dirty undershirt pushed open the trailer door with his foot and came down the steps carrying a tray of food. He was strapped with a brown leather shoulder holster holding a large, black pistol.

Branden and Robertson crouched lower into the cover of the trees and watched the man walk through the patch of light and turn the corner to the front doors of the barn. Balancing the tray on the flat of his palm, Dungarees opened one of the barn doors, stepped over the sill, and switched on an interior light. He moved toward the back of the barn and disappeared beyond the illumination of the light. Inside the barn, Robertson saw long tables holding glassware

and hotplates. He turned to Branden and whispered, "White's lab."
Branden nodded.

Robertson whispered, "I'm going closer." Just as he moved, Dungarees darted out through the barn door and ran to the trailer saying, "Jack, you need to get out here."

A second man came to the trailer door, disgruntled, and growled, "What now?"

"She's not breathing too good," Dungarees said, stopping short of the trailer. Jack came out, muttering curses, and followed Dungarees into the barn.

Robertson keyed the radio microphone clipped to the shoulder strap of his uniform, and whispered, "This is it," in mounting tension.

In short order, both men came out of the barn. Dungarees carried his tray of food back to the trailer. Jack stood under the floodlight and punched out a number on his flip phone. "It's me," he said. "Right. I don't think she can last till then. She was squawking too much, so I gagged her. Now she's puking in her gag."

Robertson drew his Sig Sauer P220 45, stepped into the clear and roared, "Stand where you are!" as Branden said, "Go. Go. Go," into a handheld radio.

Jack crouched, pulled out his pistol, and fired once in less time than it took Robertson to bring his 45 onto target. The slug clipped the sheriff on the round of his left shoulder and sprayed blood back into Branden's face.

Robertson aimed one-handed, cranked off two booming shots, and hit Jack square in the chest with both shots. As Jack toppled over, Dungarees burst through the trailer door pointing a shotgun, and Robertson shot again as deputies poured from the woods on all sides of the barn. Dungarees dropped his shotgun and raised his hands over his head. Robertson advanced angrily, his gun shaking in his right hand, as Bobby Newell threw the man to the ground and tied his hands back with a plastic loop.

Urgent shouting and a volley of shots sounded behind the barn. A deputy behind Robertson yelled "Fire!" and as he turned, the sheriff saw Branden dashing through the front doors of the barn. Two loud explosions erupted inside the barn, and flames were soon flaring out the front doors.

Robertson keyed his mic, shouted "Fire! Ambulance!" and tried to follow Branden through the doors. The flames forced him back. Ricky Niell came running around a back corner of the barn, shouting, "One perp down in back."

Robertson barked, "Two here. Branden's inside."

Niell eyed the flames and said, "There's a back door. He can get out." Robertson and Niell sprinted to the back. When they got there, the rear door was fully enveloped in flames. Sirens from a fire truck sounded out front.

At the back, Niell heard a desperate hammering on the wall of the old barn. He pulled Robertson over, and the two saw the old boards splinter outward at waist level. A booted foot kicked from inside again, and another board shattered. Holding a handkerchief to his bleeding shoulder, Robertson called men to the wall. They frantically pried away boards to open a ragged hole, and Branden handed Sara Yoder, bound hands and feet, through the opening. Then Branden pushed through, his clothes smoking, and coughed urgently, "She's choking."

Bobby Newell scooped her limp body into his muscular arms and ran for the front of the barn, flames bursting through the walls as he passed. He handed Sara to two paramedics and shouted over the din of the engines, "Choking!"

Branden limped into view, prudently several yards away from the flames that were moiling up the exterior wall of the barn. Niell came up behind him and told a paramedic, "We shot one in back," and led the paramedic to the rear.

In pain, Robertson knelt awkwardly next to Sara, beside the ambulance, and said into her ear, "You hang in there, Sara." He sat back on his haunches to watch the men working on her. One paramedic pushed deep chest compressions while the other used a vacuum hose to clear murky fluid from Sara's airway. When she opened her eyes and coughed spasmodically, the paramedic stopped the chest compressions.

They put an oxygen mask over her sooty face, rolled her onto a backboard, and hefted her into the back of the ambulance. A paramedic jumped in behind her as another closed the doors and pounded a go-ahead on the doors. The ambulance backed up, turning sharply. It pulled forward in the tight space on the lane and tried to make the turn. There wasn't enough room to make it around, so the driver put it into reverse. The backing tone sounded, and Robertson and a deputy ran down the lane, clearing a path for the ambulance.

A paramedic stopped Robertson on the lane, cut the sheriff's uniform loose over the wound, and taped a field dressing into place. Then Robertson pushed away and started after the ambulance.

As the ambulance disappeared, Branden limped up to Robertson where he had stopped at the end of the lane. "She wasn't breathing. I tore off her gag."

Robertson said, "They've got her going now, Mike. You've given her a chance."

Robertson took out his cell phone and slowly poked in the numbers for Tony Arnetto with his right thumb. When Arnetto answered, Robertson barked, "I took White's Ecstasy lab," and switched off.

Another fire truck appeared at the lane, and Branden and Robertson stepped back to let it pass. They walked back up the drive, rutted with tracks and straining fire hoses, and came as close to the burning barn as the fire chief would allow. Overhead, higher than the tops of the far trees, plumed a fiery orange glow. As Robertson knelt beside the lane, Branden took out a handkerchief, wet it in the thin spray from a fire hose linkage, and began to wipe soot and Robertson's blood off his face.

23

Sunday, July 25
6:45 A.M.

THE firefighters were hosing down smoldering hot spots in the rubble of the barn until well past dawn. Smoke and steam rose in a tall, white column into the calm, blue sky. Robertson and Branden stood beside the hissing ruins and took stock of the morning's work. Two kidnappers shot, one of them dead at the scene, the other transported to the hospital. One of their confederates captured, cuffed, and transported to the jail. Sara Yoder rescued, but perhaps not in time. No word had reached them yet of her condition.

Bobby Newell joined them, carrying a clipboard. He consulted the attached notepad and said, "We threw six shots. Am I right that three of those were yours?"

Robertson said, "Right. The first two shots hit home, and the third went wild."

Newell wrote on his notepad. When it was clear that Robertson would have nothing more to say on the matter, Newell cleared his throat and said, "Ricky shot twice and Carter once. That's three shots at the rear of the barn from our guys. The injured perp got off one shot, but I haven't got his bullet. It's probably out in the woods somewhere. Also, your third shot is not in the trailer."

"I told you," Robertson said, "my third shot went wild."

"I was just thinking you should have at least hit the trailer," Newell said, the hint of a smile lifting the corners of his mouth.

Enjoying the exchange, Branden chuckled, "Missed the trailer?"

Newell said, "I'm just saying," smiling more broadly.

Robertson said, "OK, Bobby. That's on me. One shot not recovered."

In mock puzzlement over the sheriff's reticence, Newell tapped the side of his clipboard with his pen, smiled, and ambled off toward his cruiser down the lane.

Robertson said to Branden, "I'm gonna take some ribbing about throwing a wild shot."

Branden said, "It got the job done. They'll forget it soon enough."

"I'm not so sure," Robertson said.

Ricky Niell walked over from the trailer and said, "The guy we shot out back is going to make it. He's out of surgery already."

Robertson nodded absently and surveyed the burned ruins of the barn. A few charred uprights stood in the middle of a mound of black ash and debris, all of it wet, some of it steaming. It'd take a day, maybe two, for the state fire marshal to go through the scene for evidence, but clearly the barn had been rigged to burn fast.

To Niell, Robertson said, "You heard the two explosions before he came out through the back door?"

Niell said, "At about the same time. He'd have to have thrown a switch just as he got to the back door. I figure they rigged it that way in case they were ever raided. Then he's coming at us, shooting, and the whole place went up. The back door was open, and I saw two white flashes under the long tables. After that, it was just fire everywhere, and the next thing I knew, Doc was handing Sara Yoder through a hole in the wall."

Robertson fixed his gaze on the charred ruins for a while and then said, "We'll never recover anything from the barn. They rigged it well."

"The trailer is a different story," Ricky said. "We've got ledgers and a hard drive full of contacts in Holmes and Franklin counties. I zipped up all the files, and sent them to Arnetto's office, like you asked."

"He'll be out here for the ledgers, too," Robertson said.

"We've already arrested four Holmes County dealers this morning," Ricky said. "It's been a hard morning, but we'll get the rest. Those listed on the ledgers, anyways. It'll just take a few days, is all."

Robertson toed a cinder and then crushed it under his boot. He looked around at the scene with a measure of thankfulness. Apart from him, none of his people had been hurt. Only one of the perps was dead. The action was over. The whole affair, start to finish, beginning with finding John Schlabaugh's grave and ending with Sara's rescue, had lasted only slightly more than forty hours. Robertson found himself wishing that the tension would wash out of him with the end of the action. But, he chastised himself, there were still matters to be finished. DEA agents to contend with. And one serious mistake that would trouble him for a very long time.

The firefighters were coiling their hoses and chopping at hot spots with their axes. The deputies were working the trailer, cataloging its contents. Dan Wilsher had the day-shift deputies out making arrests. With a grim satisfaction, he said, "We did some good here."

Branden answered, "If you hadn't pushed us all, Bruce, Sara would likely be dead right now."

With ire, Robertson replied, "Arnetto's just going to have to be satisfied with what he gets. I can't be worried about his problems."

Branden asked, "You called him, right?"

"Just as soon as we wrapped 'em up," Robertson said.

"Then he should have been able to raid his places in Columbus in plenty of time."

Robertson scowled, kicked at a charred board, and said, "I blew it, Mike. Dang! I blew it big time."

Branden waited.

Robertson shook his head and said, ruefully, "When I shouted 'Stand where you are,' that guy was still on his cell phone."

Branden thought briefly and then nodded. "Whoever was on the other end of that line heard us moving in."

"They will have heard the whole thing, Mike," Robertson said and produced the flip phone from his pocket. "The fool thing was still on when I picked it up."

"OK, so what's the worst scenario?"

"I'll tell you, Professor. That was Samuel Red Dog White on the line with the guy I shot. Or it was one of White's close associates. Tony Arnetto is going to show up here saying he missed White again, because I screwed up. It's going to be my fault."

"Sheriff," Branden said, "you've got to remember you saved a girl here. That's enough."

"It's going to have to be," Robertson said.

Robertson's cell phone rang and he took the call, eyes focused on the tree line overhead. He said, "Yes," listened, and then switched off. He brought his eyes to Branden's and said, "Missy. Says Sara Yoder has had a stroke. Left side paralyzed. Can't talk. She's a mess." He stood straight, slapping the cell phone into his palm, shaking his head, eyes uncertain of their focus.

Branden said, "Whatever chance she has, we gave it to her today."

Robertson said, "Tell that to her family, Mike," and walked off toward the trailer.

Branden let him go.

Bobby Newell came up as Robertson left and said to Branden, "I've never seen a place burn so fast as this one did."

Branden nodded. "I can't believe they left Sara in there to burn."

"It's not the average man who runs into a burning building," Newell commented.

Branden shrugged deprecatingly. "I'd be grateful if you didn't make too big a deal out of that."

Newell nodded, and said, "I hear on the radio that she's not doing so well."

"Possible stroke."

"She choked on her own vomit?"

"She was gagged. Threw up on the gag, and by the time I got to her, she was unconscious."

"Rough," Newell said. "We just got a radio call from Dan Wilsher. We've been able to arrest most of the Holmes County crew that was selling drugs. Arnetto ought to be plenty satisfied."

"The sheriff thinks Arnetto will probably not get his hands on Samuel White," Branden said, and explained about the flip phone.

Newell glanced down the lane and said, "By the looks of things, I'd say the sheriff was right."

Branden turned and saw Tony Arnetto stalking down the lane toward the ruins of the barn. He was slapping a radio handset forcefully against his leg and scowling an unrestrained threat. He marched up to Branden, threw his radio on the ground, and paced a tight circle in front of the professor.

Branden held his place. Robertson came heavily down the trailer steps, and Arnetto exploded into a fuming tirade of obscenities that would have made the Red Dog blush.

Robertson crowded as close to Arnetto as the man's gestures permitted, and said, "Stop this! Right now!"

Arnetto spun on Robertson and prepared to throw a punch. He didn't. Instead, he froze, his face contorted in apoplectic rage. With supreme effort, he slowly hissed, "I hope you think this was worth it."

Robertson let heat rise and fall in Arnetto, glaring back at him, his expression suggesting that he'd like it fine if Arnetto did attack him.

Branden said reasonably, "If the sheriff hadn't had us out here when he did, ready to go like we were, Sara Yoder would be dead, and you still wouldn't have Samuel White or his lab. As it is, Robertson saved a girl's life and shut down the lab to boot."

Arnetto slowly turned to face Branden and glared at him as if he hadn't had the right to speak. Branden stared back, tit for tat, and said, "Settle down, Agent Arnetto."

Bobby Newell said, "We're rounding up most of the Holmes County dealers this morning, Arnetto. Papers in the trailer told us where they are."

Arnetto stared at Newell wordlessly, as if he had only just comprehended what the captain had said, but didn't dare yet trust himself to speak.

Branden said, "The whole lab is gone. White won't be cooking X anywhere soon."

Newell said, "We have it from the Franklin County Sheriff's Department that you and they got most of White's people this morning."

Unable to calm himself, Arnetto shouted, "We did! But only because we were nearly ready to go in to make arrests ourselves. And we haven't got White. You blew it for us, Robertson!"

Robertson, still heated, backed away from Arnetto. When he had put a sensible pace or two between them, and when he could be reasonably sure that he could not strike the man, Robertson hissed, "Shut up, Arnetto!" and louder, "Shut the hell UP! You're wrong! You've been wrong all along. Because you only care about arrests. You're a disgrace to law enforcement, and I'm going to say as much in my report to your superiors. If you say ONE MORE WORD, I'm gonna lay you out cold. YOU GOT THAT?"

Heated beyond his ability to control it, Robertson nosed up to Arnetto. His face was as red as blood, and his jowls shook as anger and frustration took up residence in his muscles.

Arnetto started to say something, and Robertson seized him one-handed by the front of his suit coat, and lifted the small man to his toes. Arnetto faced the sheriff squarely, eyeball to eyeball, and didn't flinch.

Robertson felt pressure on his forearm shirtsleeve, and saw Ricky Niell pulling down on the fabric. He saw Niell's lips moving, but could not hear what the sergeant was saying. Robertson let the DEA agent down.

In a slightly milder tone, Robertson said, "Sara Yoder has had a stroke, you miserable rat. We're not sure, really, how bad off she is. But I wouldn't have waited another second, and I don't regret the decision. We did good here."

Arnetto fixed his eyes on Robertson and held them there a long time. When he had spent most of his intensity, he walked away without a further utterance.

24

PROFESSOR Branden found Sara Yoder's room in Joel Pomerene Memorial Hospital in Millersburg, on the second floor, and knocked on the half-open door as he entered. He had showered the smoke out of his hair at home and had changed into fresh clothes. A nurse was hanging a new IV bag on the stand beside Sara's bed. Albert O. Yoder and Martha Yoder were seated on chairs in the corner by the head of Sara's bed. Martha had reached her arm through the bars at the side of the bed and lovingly stroked Sara's long black hair. Cal Troyer stood at the foot of the bed and, as Branden entered the room, put his finger to his lips for silence.

Branden acknowledged the Yoders and whispered in Cal's ear, "How's she doing?"

Cal led the professor out into the hall and said, "She's not good. If she can't quickly recover most of her motor skills in the next several weeks, the damage could be permanent."

"Can she talk at all?" Branden asked.

"Not well. Some words come out OK, and others stall on her lips. The left side of her face is mostly immobile, and she struggles to say what little she can manage."

"Is that what the doctors said? That she could have permanent damage?"

"They said they'll know in a few days. What doesn't come back then will be an indication of how bad it is. The rest will take long months of therapy, and she might not ever get it all back."

Martha Yoder, Sara's mother, came out into the hall, her long wine-red dress rustling as she moved. To Branden, she said, "Thank you for saving her, Professor Branden. Truly God has provided you as a miracle."

Branden said, "I wouldn't go that far, Mrs. Yoder."

"We know miracles when we see them, Professor. We also understand tragedy. God works in our lives in all ways, and we accept His wisdom. In this case, we are grateful for His mercy, even if His instrument doesn't comprehend what he has done. We thank you, Professor, for being God's instrument."

Blushing, Branden managed to say, "You are welcome."

Sara's father came out of the room and said, "She wants to see you, Professor."

Branden eyed Cal with a self-conscious modesty, and Cal tipped his head toward Sara's room. Branden slipped into the room alone and stood beside the head of Sara's bed. He leaned over with his elbows on the railing, putting his face close to hers.

Sara lifted her head off the pillow, straining at the shoulders, and struggled for words. She formed her lips several times before she managed the one word, "Prayed." Then, "They all prayed."

Branden took her hand and said, "Yes. A great many people, Sara. Prayed through the night. For your safety. For your rescue."

Sara said with difficulty, "You . . . came . . . saved . . . "

"We all did, Sara. The sheriff and his deputies. The firefighters and ambulance squad. The night dispatcher. It wasn't just me."

"Thank . . . all . . . " she uttered, exhausted, and sank back onto her pillow.

Outside her room, in the hall, Branden found that Bishop Raber had joined Cal and the Yoders. Raber was in the middle of saying, "Your horse has been standing there a long time. I gave it water. You should go home, rest. Put your horse up properly."

Martha said earnestly, "Oh, I can't leave, Bischoff."

"I'll sit with her," Raber said. "Albert, the two of you go home and get some rest. You've been up all night."

Albert O. Yoder agreed reluctantly, and Martha followed Albert's lead. They slipped into Sara's room and came out shortly, Martha carrying an overnight bag of a flowered corduroy fabric, and Albert carrying a brown paper sack of groceries. To Raber, Albert said, "Do you want to keep the food?"

Raber took Albert's arm at the elbow and led him down the hall. "My wife will bring supper," he said, and ushered the two Yoders to the stairwell. There Albert stalled, handed the grocery bag to Raber, and returned to Branden and Troyer. With tears in his eyes, he said, "We take life as it comes to us. Handicaps are just part of life," and seemed, then, to freeze in place, paralyzed by sorrow and loss.

Bishop Raber came up to him and led him back to the stairwell, down the steps, and out to the hitching rail where their horse was tied. When the bishop regained the second-floor hallway outside Sara's room, he said to Branden and Cal, "They lost a child in a riding accident three years ago. Now they're worried they'll lose Sara, too." He went into Sara's room and sat at the head of her bed.

Outside, Cal said to Branden, "Missy told me that Bruce says Agent Arnetto and the Columbus police have not been able to arrest this Samuel White."

"They haven't, so far as I know."

"Then I think that compromises the safety of at least three kids: Abe, Jeremiah, and Sara."

"They're all at risk. The sooner we get him, the better for all of them."

"Missy also told me that Bruce doesn't plan on holding Jeremiah on charges."

"I don't know about that," Branden said.

"You don't know, or you don't concur?"

"I don't know what Bruce has in mind for Jeremiah. He hasn't been charged with a crime. He hasn't committed one, so far as I know. What are you getting at, Cal?"

"Mike, I think you and I should go down to Columbus to talk with Abe Yoder in the hospital. It's time we found out once and for all what has really been going on with these kids."

25

THE Franklin County sheriff's deputy on duty outside Abe Yoder's hospital room took Cal Troyer's clergy identification and Professor Branden's reserve sheriff deputy's credentials, and then told them to take seats against the wall. He made a call on a cell phone, read the credentials out loud, switched off, and made an entry in a logbook he kept in his uniform shirt pocket. He waved Branden and Troyer over, opened Abe Yoder's door, and closed it again when they were inside.

Abe Yoder's bed was raised so that he lay level with Branden's chest. An IV bag fed a line into Abe's left wrist. Abe, naked above the waist, was propped with pillows onto his right side, and a large bandage was taped to his left side. He was sleeping lightly, his left hand clasping the aluminum safety rail. When Branden went up to him, he opened his eyes and closed them again. He pulled his pillow down a bit, repositioned his head, and opened his eyes. He saw Cal Troyer at Branden's side, and said, "Hello, Pastor," in a hoarse whisper.

Cal moved closer and said, "We need to talk to you, Abe. Can you wake up for a while?"

Abe nodded and pulled on the safety rail to bring himself closer to the edge of the bed. To Branden, he said, "We met once before, but I can't remember. The bar?"

"Yes," Branden said, "and I found you at the cabin where you were hiding."

Yoder nodded with effort and said, "Is there any ice?"

Cal poured out some ice water from a pink plastic pitcher and drained most of the water into a sink in the corner of the room. Back at Abe's side, he spooned a chip of ice into Yoder's mouth, and Yoder mumbled something approximating "Thank you" around the ice.

When he had finished chewing, Yoder asked, "Has anyone found Sara?"

Branden said, "We found her last night, Abe."

Yoder asked, "She OK?"

"She's safe," Branden said, "but there are complications. She's in Pomerene Hospital."

Abe closed his eyes, worked his jaw muscles, said, "Jeremiah?" and opened his eyes. His hand began to tremble on the safety rail.

"He's with the sheriff," Cal said.

A nurse came into the room and put a thermometer in Yoder's ear. Then she checked his pulse against her wristwatch.

"How is he?" Branden asked.

"His temperature is coming down," she said. "Pulse is too high still."

"What do the doctors say about his infection?" Cal asked.

"As long as his temperature keeps coming down, they're not too worried," she said. At the door, she turned and said, "He knows to push his button if he needs more pain medication."

Abe said, "I can't find the button."

Branden fished a gray wire out from between the safety rail and the bed frame. He looped it over the railing so that the red button was within easy reach. To Yoder, he said, "Can you wait on that medication, Abe? We need to ask you some questions."

Yoder said, "A little while, I guess. It really hurts. You need to keep Jeremiah out of trouble. He's better off in jail now than running loose."

Branden asked, "Why is that, Abe?"

"He might try to go after that guy White. Because of Sara."

"Does he know how to contact White?" Cal asked.

"I gave him a number to call. And then White called on Johnny's prepaid phone."

Branden said, "We know about that, Abe. Sara is safe. There's no reason for Jeremiah to do anything to White, now. What you need to do is to tell us everything that has happened. The drugs. Samuel White. John Schlabaugh."

At the name Schlabaugh, Yoder clenched his eyes shut and pushed on the railing to move back from the professor. Branden leaned in closer, and said, "Who shot John Schlabaugh?"

In obvious torment, Abe said, "White."

"Why?" Branden asked.

"Over the drugs."

"You have to tell us the whole story, Abe," Branden insisted.

Yoder opened his eyes and motioned to Cal for some more ice. He took the cup, knocked some ice into his mouth, and crunched it between his teeth. He repeated that until all the ice was gone from the cup, and then handed the cup back to Troyer and sighed heavily, turning his head from side to side. Then he started talking softly, so that Branden and Troyer had to move closer to hear.

"White came out with some of his men a couple of weeks after we took the drugs, and he wanted his money. Right then and there. It was me, John Schlabaugh, and Andy Stutzman, and we met White and his men at the red barn. Andy was crazy drunk like he always is, and me and John talked to White. We hadn't sold hardly any of the drugs, so he hit Johnny and beat him up. We wanted to give all of what was left back to him, but White wouldn't let us. He said we owed him cash for the drugs and if we didn't pay up, he'd kill one of us.

"That's when Johnny started talking fast. He told White about old Spits Wallace and his gold coins. Everybody knows about that. Johnny said he'd show White how to find the Wallace place, if he'd just let us go. Just let us have more time to sell the drugs, and White could have the gold coins in the meantime.

"When we got to the Wallace place, Andy was passed out in the back of the SUV White was driving. We thought we could just bust in there and grab the gold. That's when one of White's guys got shot. Going in the kitchen door. We never saw Wallace, but he must have shot the guy. White started screaming at us. He hit Johnny with his gun, and while he was hitting Johnny, I took off running, and I heard a shot. I didn't feel a bullet. Heard the shot, but didn't feel anything until later.

"They had Andy in the back, and I saw them stuff Johnny in the car too, and load that dead guy in the back. I had a feeling they'd go back to the red barn, so I started off through the woods to get there, and my side was starting to hurt, so I touched it down there and got blood on my hand. When I got to the edge of the woods above the barn, I had a good view from about fifty yards away, and I stayed hidden behind the trees. They had Andy hauled out on his stomach in the dirt and Johnny kneeling in the gravel beside him. White had a gun out, and I thought Andy and John was both goners for sure."

As he spoke, Abe Yoder's eyes widened to saucers. His grip on the aluminum safety rail tightened, and his hand shook spasmodically under the strain.

Cal said, "Take it easy, Abe," and handed him another cup of ice.

Yoder chewed, and drew in ragged breaths. Puddles gathered in his eyes, and tears began to stream down his cheeks.

"I ran away when Johnny needed me," he said, sobbing. "I ran away to save myself. Oh, Johnny! I couldn't save you. Oh, God help me! I can't stand it."

As Branden and Troyer tried to calm Yoder, his IV line pulled loose, and the pump alarm started beeping. A nurse ran in and rushed up to Yoder's side. She shut off the IV pump, pushed Branden and Troyer back a bit, and examined the dressing over Yoder's wound. A second nurse came in and demanded, "Under control?"

First Nurse said, "His line pulled loose. I'll have it reinserted in a minute."

Second Nurse scolded Branden and Troyer, "You can't disturb Mr. Yoder. You'll have to leave if you're going to rile him up."

Troyer said, "We'll be fine. The worst is over."

Second Nurse eyed him skeptically and waited for the first nurse to finish attaching the IV needle to a second spot on Yoder's wrist. When the first nurse walked out, Second Nurse said, "You'll have to leave if he gets agitated again."

Branden and Troyer nodded silently, and she left. When they returned to his side, Abe was calmer. He started talking on his own.

"I couldn't hear what White was saying, but he was angry. He yelled a lot, and Johnny just knelt there, with his head hanging down. Then White went over and hauled Andy up onto his knees. Left him swaying there, drunk like he was. Anyway, I don't know what he said, but White laughed, stepped back, and leveled that big black gun at Andy. Andy lurched forward, White cocked the hammer back, and that's when Johnny lunged at him. To try to stop him from killing Andy. Johnny Schlabaugh got shot in the head trying to save Andy Stutzman, and all White did was laugh about it. He left Andy kneeling in the dirt, and drove away. He left Johnny sprawled out on the gravel, dead.

"When I got down to them, Andy was sobered up some. He was knelt over Johnny's body, crying. Moaning some horrible sound, like a tortured animal. I couldn't get him to shut up. He must have been out of his mind. Then, all of a sudden, Andy stumbled up onto his feet, and started running down the lane. Like he was chased by demons. I tried to find him later, but he must have cut through the woods, because I never saw him again. All I could think of was that me and Johnny had a fight the night before, and he bloodied my nose. Him lying there dead, and all I could think about was some stupid fight.

"I buried Johnny as deep as I could. My side was hurting, and I passed out once. I took his secret, prepaid phone because I thought it would be safer to use than mine. I hid in the cabin. Tried to heal up the wound from where they shot me. I called Jeremiah, and he came to help me. Then we got worried. They can trace those phones. We saw that on TV. I couldn't let White trace me while I couldn't move, so I let Jeremiah take Johnny's phone. I told him to throw it away.

"Before, when I still had Johnny's phone, I put a message in the *Sugarcreek Budget,* and I was planning on getting away from there. I was going to be long gone before anyone could figure out that message. I didn't even know they would see it, the rest of the gang, but everybody reads the *Budget,* so I thought—Oh—I don't know what I thought. I couldn't leave Johnny in that hole in the ground without letting somebody know where he was. And I couldn't stand the idea of telling Jeremiah face to face what had happened. I thought I could get away. Not have to face any of them."

"You just buried him and left?" Cal asked.

Abe said, "I didn't know what else to do. I still had the drugs and a lot of money. If I told about Johnny, the sheriff would find out, and then I'd never get a chance to settle up with White. We'd all have been in danger. Guys like White can find people easy enough. I thought if I had more time, I could do something. But I barely made it back to the cabins. Then I felt bad about it, and I put that message in the *Budget.*"

"How did you think anyone would find Johnny's body?" Cal asked.

Abe closed his eyes, sighed heavily. "I can't remember. I was passed out half the time. Jeremiah helped me, but I never told him about Johnny. I guess I figured I'd be long gone by the time the *Budget* came out on Wednesday.

"But I got worse in my side, and I started losing track of the time. Couldn't travel. I don't remember how I got in the hospital."

"I found you, Abe," Branden said. "We took you to the hospital. By then, Sara had led us to John Schlabaugh."

Yoder drew in a labored breath and sighed it out slowly.

Branden asked, "Did Jeremiah take you out of the hospital?"

Yoder nodded and said, "He was crazy about Sara. Said we had to give the briefcase back to get Sara free. He said White had called him on Johnny's prepaid cell phone, Friday morning, and said he was going to kill her if we didn't show up with the drugs or the money. He said he was cutting his losses now that Johnny was dead. Said he couldn't trust the rest of us hillbillies to make good on the sale of his drugs, so he'd take all the cash and all the drugs we still had."

"You didn't know we had found the briefcase," Branden said.

"No. And then we were just crazy people. Went down to that bar. We didn't know what we were doing. We couldn't give the drugs back anymore. So, we had to try something."

"Sara is safe now," Cal said, reassuringly.

Yoder squeezed his eyelids together and sobbed.

Branden dried Abe's cheeks with the edge of the bedsheets. Cal wet a towel from the bathroom and placed it on Abe Yoder's forehead. When Yoder got himself composed, he whispered, "Stop Jeremiah."

26

Sunday, July 25
7:40 P.M.

IN ROBERTSON'S office later, Jeremiah sat in front of Robertson's big desk in the same English clothes he had worn at the bar the day before and sulked. Branden sat facing him, and Robertson stood behind his desk. Jeremiah steadfastly refused to talk about either his activities or his intentions.

Robertson said, "If I could charge you with something, Jeremiah, I'd do that. Just to keep you here."

"You haven't got a reason to keep me," Jeremiah said. "And I don't want to stay."

Robertson said to Branden, "You try something."

Branden said, "We'll get him, Jeremiah. All you have to do is trust us."

"Abe told me White killed Johnny Schlabaugh," Jeremiah stated flatly. "And he tried to kill Sara. What would you do with him if you did catch him?"

Robertson said, "He'd go to trial. Probably get life in prison."

Jeremiah shook his head and focused his eyes on the front of Robertson's desk. "I don't know where he is," he said. "I'm not going to do anything stupid."

"Look, young man," Robertson said aggressively, not believing Jeremiah. "I won't have you running off half-cocked to try to handle this on your own."

Jeremiah said, "I'm just one kid. How am I going to handle a guy like this White?"

"Listen good," Robertson said. "If something happens to White outside of the law, I'm coming after you!"

"What can the law do?" Jeremiah asked. "This White gets away all the time!"

"His people are locked up," Robertson said, forcing some calm into his voice. "We got them, Jeremiah. They're not getting off. And the same will happen to Samuel White. It's just a matter of time."

Jeremiah didn't respond. Instead, he looked to Branden with a question in his eyes.

Branden said, "You can trust the sheriff, Jeremiah. Let the authorities handle this. Go see Sara. I'm sure she can use the company. Stay out of the hunt for White. Go home and sit a while with Gertie. You deserve some peace in your life. Make a life with Sara. She needs someone like you. Don't let her down, now. Let it rest."

Jeremiah pondered the matter as he sat immobile in his chair. He closed his eyes and drew a long breath. He turned and studied the professor's eyes for a long time, and saw a sure, peaceful conviction there. He nodded, got up, and said, "OK." Then he turned to Robertson and said, "Can I go now?"

Robertson's expression was skeptical, but he said, "Sure, Jeremiah. We can't hold you."

Jeremiah walked to the door, turned, and said, "I'm going to see Sara, and then I'm going away for a few days. Is that going to be a problem?"

"No problem," Robertson said. "You're free to go. But I'm warning you. Don't blow this now."

Jeremiah looked steadily to each man, turned, and walked out.

Robertson sat down at his desk, took a pencil, and tapped the eraser end nervously on his desktop. Branden lounged in the low leather chair to the right of Robertson's desk, feet out straight and crossed at the ankles, fingertips snatching nervously at his short beard.

Robertson said, "That kid's gonna go after White."

"I know," Branden said. "We've got to figure a way to get to White first."

Bobby Newell, in uniform, came into the office holding a printout and said, "We've got a preliminary report from the BCI lab people on Schlabaugh's Firebird. I asked them to come out a day early. Work a Sunday. They lifted seven prints. None are in the system. The blood on the driver's seat matches Abe Yoder's type, but it'll take a while if we want DNA matching."

"We know Abe moved the Firebird," Branden said. "Parked it in the barn. That's going to have been after he got shot."

"So no DNA?" Newell asked.

"Not at the moment," Robertson said. "How about Abe Yoder's phone? The one from the grave?"

"Dan had the phone company print out the calls and messages earlier today. It's apparently all innocuous stuff."

Branden said, "It has all the numbers stored?"

"All the times, and all the numbers," Newell said.

"Then one of them is going to be Jeremiah Miller's cell phone," Branden said. "Another will be Johnny Schlabaugh's."

"I suppose so," Newell said.

"Can the phone company tell us if Jeremiah makes a call on either of those phones?" Branden asked.

"Yes," Newell said. "They can tell us when he makes a call, and what his location is."

"So, that's a way to keep track of where he is when he makes a call," Branden said.

Robertson asked, "Can they record the conversations?"

Newell said, "They can get text messages. I don't know about voice."

Robertson said, "Then let's follow this up, Bobby. On your night shift, and Dan Wilsher, tomorrow. If he makes a call, we need to know where he is, and what he's saying, if that's possible. We especially need to know who he's calling. And text messages he sends."

Newell said, "I'll get a warrant," and left.

Branden pushed himself out of his chair and paced in front of Robertson's desk. "Is this the best we can do?" he asked.

"If we follow Jeremiah around," Robertson said, "he's either going to rabbit on us or lay low. Wait us out."

"Maybe that wouldn't be so bad."

There was a knock at the door, and the night-shift dispatcher, Ed Hollings, came in and said, "Sheriff, you have a visitor."

Tony Arnetto pushed past Hollings into the office and walked a slow, deliberate circle in front of the tall office windows. Hollings shrugged, turned, and left.

Robertson asked, "Have you got White yet?"

Arnetto ignored the question. "I want to talk to the kid you brought in with Abe Yoder. Jeremiah something."

"Miller," Branden said. "Jeremiah Miller."

"Well, good for him!" Arnetto shot. "He's a Miller. How very special."

"We let him go," Robertson said, rising from his desk chair.

Arnetto threw his arms in the air and glared spitefully at the sheriff.

"He's gone," Robertson said. "No charges."

Arnetto cracked a sarcastic smile and said, "You've got two kids in the hospital, one in the morgue, and you let the only one who can help us go? That's great, Sheriff! Commendable."

Branden saw Robertson start out around his desk, and he bolted to his feet and blocked the sheriff at the front corner of his desk. Robertson glowered at Arnetto, gained control of himself with difficulty, and turned back to his seat, saying, "He hasn't done anything, Arnetto. I don't throw kids in lockup on a whim."

Arnetto took his suit coat off and laid it over his arm with exaggerated calm. Scowling, he said, "Have you at least kept hold of the men from the barn bust?"

Robertson mastered his tone. "We've got a Dick DiPaldi upstairs.

He was captured coming out of the trailer. And we've got John Albert under guard at the hospital."

Arnetto said, arrogantly, "I'll talk to DiPaldi first."

Robertson punched his intercom button and said, "Ed, Agent Arnetto is to go up to the cell blocks. Set him up with DiPaldi."

Hollings said, "OK," and soon appeared in Robertson's doorway.

Robertson gestured for Arnetto to follow Hollings, and the DEA agent stalked out of the office. Hollings lingered in the doorway, shaking his head, and Robertson said, "Don't take any crap off that guy."

Hollings smiled and left, closing the door.

When Robertson was seated again, Branden said, "So, what's our plan?"

Robertson said, "We'll see what the phone company can do with calls made on Jeremiah's phones."

"And if Jeremiah goes down to Columbus?"

"I don't know," Robertson said, dissatisfied.

"And if Jeremiah doesn't go down to Columbus?"

"I don't know," Robertson said again, dispirited.

"The best thing would be if Jeremiah just stays put," Branden said.

"The best thing would be if none of this had ever happened."

WEDNESDAY, JULY 28

27

Wednesday, July 28
2:15 P.M.

THREE days later, Caroline and Michael Branden drove up to the high ridge at Saltillo under low, dull, nickel-colored skies. They traveled through a steady, warm drizzle as they crossed down into the little valley where Albert O. and Martha Yoder had their sprawling farm, straddling a gravel lane that bisected the valley. The professor parked next to Cal Troyer's gray truck, and he and Caroline walked up the driveway, sharing a black umbrella. Ascending the steps to a front porch that stretched the full width of the two-story white frame house, they found Cal seated with several Amish men. Caroline inquired about Mrs. Yoder and was directed inside, to the kitchen. The professor leaned back against the porch railing and listened to the conversation, a running debate about modern tractors and slow draft horses. The men all wore cream-colored straw hats and sported chin whiskers, shaved smooth around the mouth. Most of the whiskers were white or gray. These were the older men, not needed for the afternoon on the farms. Two of the men smoked: one a pipe and the other a cigarette that he had rolled himself. At a break in the discussion, Branden asked about Sara and was told they still expected her home this afternoon. She was supposed to be released after lunch. The change in subject seemed to bring the debate about tractors to a conclusion, and the men fell silent.

Branden excused himself and went into the house, back along a narrow hallway, to the warm kitchen. There, several women worked at a black, cast-iron woodstove, sliding pies in to bake and taking out the ones that were done. Caroline had put on an apron and was peeling apples at the sink.

In a corner next to a worktable, Albert O. Yoder sat on a Shaker chair, vigorously turning the hand crank of an old wooden ice cream maker, sweat beading on his brow. Branden offered assistance, switched places with Albert, and began turning the stubborn crank. Albert leaned over the sink, got a drink from the spigot of a red hand pump, and then wet his handkerchief and used it to wipe his face and neck.

Martha Yoder stood next to Caroline at the sink, topping and slicing strawberries. She carried a bowl to Branden at the ice cream maker and had him open the top so that she could pour in her strawberries. Then she cut two Dutch apple pies while they were still warm, put a piece on each of five plates, and carried them on a platter out to the front porch. A neighbor lady carried out a tray with napkins, forks, and glasses of fresh whole milk.

Albert took over the crank on the ice cream maker, and Branden strolled out onto the back screened porch. Oblivious to the drizzling rain, a half dozen young children in either denim trousers or full-length dresses were intent on a game of tag that centered on a tall wooden swing set and spilled out of the backyard toward the barn at the side of the house. In front of the barn doors, Branden found six buggies, hitched to hobbled horses. A lad of about fourteen was carrying hay to the horses, and his sister, about ten, toted a bucket of water to one horse and lifted it high on her short arms to let the horse drink.

Branden cut in among the buggies and entered the dark and cool barn. In stalls along an inside wall, two boys were milking goats. The game of tag came too near them, and one of the milkers gently scolded the younger children away from the temperamental animals.

The kids ran out the opposite barn doors, splashing their bare feet in a mud puddle as they left. Branden paced the distance inside the barn, enjoying the aromas of straw and fresh-cut hay. He followed the children out the opposite side of the barn and walked around to the front porch again. He took an empty seat as one of the men was saying, "It'll be a shame if she's got permanent damage."

Cal answered, "She seemed a little better to me yesterday."

The men nodded solemnly. The pipe smoker knocked out his ashes over the porch railing.

Albert O. Yoder came out through the screened door rubbing at his cranking arm. He said, "Ice cream's ready, if you care for some."

Two of the men nodded, got up, and went inside. Albert O. sat next to Professor Branden, saying, "I thought they'd be here by now."

Branden said, "The roads are kind of muddy. They'll be along soon."

Cal said, "I think they're here now," and pointed down the lane.

Jeremiah Miller drove a tall, proud, Standardbred horse hitched to a big, black, two-seater buggy. The seat beside him was unoccupied. He proceeded down the gravel lane slowly, negotiating the potholes and ruts with careful attention to minimize the jostling the rig took. There was a shout from one of the children, and the game of tag stopped, the little ones filing out to the front driveway. Albert called in through the screened door, and the women in the kitchen came out onto the porch.

Jeremiah pulled up on the lawn, close to the front porch, and jumped down from the buggy. He was dressed in his Sunday best suit. The formerly crisp lines of his fanciful beard were fading with new growth on his cheeks, trimmed to the traditional chin whiskers, and shaved around the mouth, Amish style. The thin and rakish beard and mustache that had been his statement of youthful identity, the thing that set him apart from the *Gemie,* were a mark of the Rumschpringe. Until he joined the church, this stubborn act of rebellion had been tolerated in the community. Now that he had given himself an Amish shave, he was known to have identified properly with the church.

He waved some of the men down from the porch. Four of them gathered at the back of the buggy. Together, they rolled Sara Yoder's wheelchair to the edge and then lifted her and her chair gently down. An umbrella popped open over Sara, and Jeremiah began to roll her over the grass, toward the front porch.

One of the youngest children shyly said, "Hi, Sara," and the others watched quietly. The men and women stood expectantly on the front porch and watched her approach. She was leaning heavily left in the chair, and her face was slack on the left side, eyes watery. When they lifted her up to the front porch, she held her left hand immobile in her lap, and reached out to take her mother's hand with her right. Martha knelt beside Sara's chair and kissed her on the cheek. Sara awkwardly mouthed the words, "I am tired," and Martha wheeled her over the threshold. Albert met them in the front hallway and scooped Sara up into his arms, to carry her to her up-stairs bedroom. Jeremiah stood, hat in hand, and watched through the screened door. When Albert came back down, Jeremiah and he stepped into the parlor for a private talk.

On the front yard, the game of tag started up again. The milkers came out of the barn, each carrying two pails of goat's milk, and walked around to the back porch. One of the neighbor ladies served ice cream out of a large bowl, and the men on the front porch sat back down where they had been seated earlier.

Little was said. Very little needed to be said. To everyone assembled there, it was apparent that Sara had struggled mightily to keep herself upright in her wheelchair. She had mumbled the few words she had spoken. It was unclear whether her face would ever show a convincing smile again.

When Albert and Jeremiah came out, they were allowed to sit quietly with the men. They were not pressed into conversation. Eventually, Jeremiah said his sad good-byes and turned his buggy to go back down the lane toward home. Caroline came out and nodded to the professor that they should leave. Cal walked them out to their car, but said nothing beyond his thanks that they had come out that afternoon.

Down the lane, Bishop Raber's buggy came into view. Raber stopped when Jeremiah came alongside, and the two men spoke for a while, out of earshot.

When the lane was clear, Caroline and the professor drove toward home. The bishop had gone into the house, and most of the visitors had begun preparing their buggies for their trips home. In the space of an hour, the Yoder family found themselves alone with their sorrows, as Sara slept upstairs.

FRIDAY, JULY 30

28

Friday, July 30
9:00 A.M.

JOHN SCHLABAUGH was buried on the high ground at Salem Cemetery, under a towering blue morning sky. The whole congregation tended to the physical and spiritual needs of the Schlabaugh family, who alone sat in chairs, in a fluttering breeze, beside the grave. Cal Troyer and Michael and Caroline Branden attended the subdued services, and Jeremiah Miller brought Sara Yoder in her wheelchair. Abe Yoder was still in the Columbus hospital. Of the remaining members of the Schlabaugh Rumschpringe gang, only Ben Troyer and John Miller attended. Mary Troyer had taken a buggy to visit relatives up in Middlefield, and Henry Erb had left on a bus for Kansas. Andy Stutzman was conspicuously absent.

The first preacher handled the remarks at the graveside, emphasizing Psalm 139 and God's refusal to abandon his children. Bishop Raber presided over interring the body. A longer service was later conducted in Albert O. and Martha Yoder's barn, with martyr hymns sung a cappella, the second preacher giving forth for an hour and a half on the subject of forgiveness.

After the services, a large noon meal was served on the lawns of the Yoder house, both in front of the big house and between the house and barn, in order to accommodate the large number of people. Long tables were set up under canopies to ward off the sun. The women prepared the meal and first served the men, seated on deacon's benches pulled up to the tables. The women went about their preparations calmly, carrying platters of roast beef and fried chicken, potatoes, buttered beans, and coleslaw from the bustling kitchen to the outdoor tables. When the men had eaten and the first round of dishes had been washed, the women sat down to eat. The men gathered in small groups, inside and outside, to talk.

During the men's meal, Cal Troyer and Michael Branden sat together, across from Bishop Raber. Caroline helped the women serve and then ate with them. Jeremiah Miller ate with Sara Yoder, in the front parlor, when the women were served.

The smallest children of the congregation played on the swing set and trampoline in the backyard, and sent emissaries periodically to check on Sara and Jeremiah, the little ones unable to mask their curiosity about romance or silence their giggles. Older children gathered behind the black buggies parked up and down the lane, and whispered about the high drama of the Schlabaugh Rumschpringe gang. Cigarettes and a jug of last year's plum wine were passed secretly among the oldest.

As the last dishes were being cleared from the tables, the people heard the loud revving of a car engine from some distance up the lane, and an old, brown Chevette lurched into view, weaving erratically, gears grinding out painfully as Andy Stutzman fumbled the gear shifter and the clutch. Too fast for caution, he drove the Chevette up to the line of buggies and slid sideways in the gravel to an abrupt halt. Andy stumbled out of the little car in formal Amish attire, a Sunday suit, and fell over onto his hands and knees, clutching a longneck beer bottle by the throat. With difficulty, he cranked his limbs upright, took a long pull on the bottle, and threw it off into the weeds beside the road.

He brought his eyes angrily into focus on the people standing in front of the house, and forced himself into a stumbling march across the lawn.

Andy's father stepped forward, laid his hand on Andy's shoulder, and said, "That's enough, now. Go home."

Andy pushed his father away and glared at the people. The younger children were gathered up quietly and taken into the house by their mothers.

Andy waved belligerently in the space in front of his face and blurted, "You've got no right! None of you!"

His father tried again to restrain him, but Andy pushed him off and stumbled backward. He wiped his sleeve across his lips and yelled, "Johnny Schlabaugh knew more about living than all you clodhoppers put together. You are not worthy to mourn him! Hypocrites!"

Andy hoisted both arms over his head and threw them to his side in drunken frustration. He skittered sideways on the lawn, lost his footing, and fell over on his side. He lay, curled up, mumbling, until Jeremiah and John Miller came down off the porch, picked him up, and carried him, unconscious, into the barn. They laid him on some loose straw in one of the stalls, and when they came out, the people were starting to move again and to talk. In time, everyone seemed to settle back to normal.

Bishop Raber drew Andy's father aside and asked, "Can you get him home?"

Stutzman nodded wordlessly, eyes cast to the ground, obviously deeply embarrassed.

Raber said, "I'll have some men load him into your buggy in a bit."

Stutzman nodded again, hesitated, and said, "We're afraid of him, Bischoff. He hurts people when he's drunk."

"Has he hit you?"

"Yes."

"Has he hit your wife?"

"No."

"Has he broken things?"

"All over the house."

"Why didn't you say something to me?"

A humiliated shrug.

"We've got to do something."

"What? He is our son."

"The preachers and I need to make a decision about him," Raber said solemnly. "You need to prepare yourself for the worst."

"He's planning to leave us. It'll break his mother's heart, Bischoff."

"I know that well enough," Raber said gently. "But isn't her heart breaking now, anyway?"

* * *

In the slow afternoon, before the women ate their traditional meal separate from and after the men, Jeremiah was able to coax Sara up onto crutches long enough to move out onto the front porch. She leaned on her crutches for several minutes, gratefully watching the youngsters run a marauding game of tag, and then asked for her wheelchair. Jeremiah wheeled the chair out to her, and they returned to the parlor.

When the women had finished eating and had washed up another stack of dishes, it was announced that pie would be served off the back porch. The men made it slowly around to the back and stood in line with the younger children for their pie. Cal Troyer took two plates to Jeremiah and Sara in the parlor, and sat with them while Jeremiah helped Sara eat and then finished his own pie.

Sara managed a "Thank you" of sorts.

Cal nodded and put the empty plates on an oil-lamp stand in the corner of the parlor. He sat back down, saying, "You're doing better, Sara."

She smiled crookedly, the muscles on her left side not quite cooperating with the right side of her face. She looked to Jeremiah and then to Cal and said, "It's slow."

Cal said, "I talked with Abe Yoder yesterday, down at Mt. Carmel East Hospital. He looks better. Should be released soon."

Jeremiah said, "I suppose you've heard about Johnny's things. His property."

Cal shook his head and said, "What about them?"

"The Schlabaughs have agreed to sell everything, tractor and all, to raise money. So the church can buy more land close to here. The men will all help to raise a cash crop each year, so the Bishop will have funds he can use when someone needs a doctor."

Cal said, "That's all in the future. What about now? Are you two going to be all right?"

Sara gave Jeremiah another of her crooked smiles and said to Cal, "Be fine."

Jeremiah followed with his own enigmatic smile and said, "You don't need to worry about us one bit."

Cal said, "If it was just the two of you, I wouldn't worry. But with Red Dog White still running loose, that gives me cause to worry a lot."

Jeremiah leveled his eyes at the pastor and said, "You also do not need to worry about him."

* * *

As most of the congregation was preparing to leave, Cal took the opportunity to sit in the parlor again with Sara and Jeremiah. Sara cradled her left forearm in her right hand and lifted her left arm as high as she could manage, about level with her earlobes. Jeremiah helped her hold it there for several seconds and then lowered her arm to her lap. They exercised the limb that way several times, and Sara said to Cal, "Supposed to keep moving."

Her enunciation of the letter "v" in "moving" produced an awkward "w" sound. She said, "Moving," again, and struggled to get a better "v," this time coming closer to the correct pronunciation.

Cal encouraged her, saying, "If you keep at it, Sara, you'll come along faster. The key is to keep trying."

Sara nodded sternly and let her left arm settle into her lap. She held Cal's eyes for a spell, turned aside and said, softly, struggling for some of the words, and watching Jeremiah's eyes, "Jeremiah wants to marry me."

"He's a fine young man," Cal answered.

"Got land," Sara said.

Jeremiah explained, "Usually, it's the land that holds a couple back. Land is so expensive. But, I've got our land all set up. My uncles have set a tract aside for me when I marry."

"You'll have to make some changes," Cal said.

"We've already allowed so many accommodations to modern things," Jeremiah said. "There are batteries under buggies for radios and lights, and cell phones everywhere. Johnny used to say we were all hypocrites. That we'd accept some things and reject others, without any consistency, without any sensible reasons. Hypocrites, Cal. That's what he would say if he were still alive. How can we be sure what is right?"

Cal offered, "Only the Schwartzentruber sect is still completely backward. Can you all be Schwartzentrubers?"

"I couldn't live like that, so close to the earth," Jeremiah said. "But it's the temptation that drives you mad, Cal. You think the English have such wonderful things. Turns out all they have is gadgets. If Johnny showed me anything, it's that gadgets can't make you happy."

"So, you're both ready to live Amish?" Cal asked, looking from one to the other.

Jeremiah said, "I am," and glanced knowingly at Sara.

Cal said to Sara, "But?"

Sara tried for a sentence and failed. Eventually she managed, "Lose me. Lose Sara."

Jeremiah took her hand and explained for her. "She'd lose herself, her identity. She'd be swallowed up in conformity, and who she could have been would fade with the years into something indistinguishable from the hundred other Amish women who have tied their lives to a bishop, a husband, the church. She'd lose herself, Cal. We've talked about this before. Right, Sara?"

Sara nodded.

Cal sat and pondered this, while his fingers brushed across his short white beard. He nodded seriously, then smiled and said to Sara, "You don't know why God numbers the hairs on your head."

Sara looked puzzled. She waited for him to explain.

Cal said, "In the scriptures, it states that God knows us so well that He has counted the hairs on each of our heads."

Sara gave a lopsided nod, still puzzled.

"It's not a statement about what God does. It's not even about hair, really. It's a statement about God's capacity to know us, and recognize us, as individuals, Sara."

"Amish—all—same."

"Aren't you Sara Yoder?"

A cautious nod.

"How many Sara Yoders are there who were born on your birthday, to your parents?"

"Just me."

"Then this alone makes you unique. There is no one like you. There never can be. God's ability to know you, to recognize you, and to acknowledge you as an individual is infinite. That's what that scripture means."

"I don't see how that can be possible," Jeremiah said. "All Amish are the same. Indistinguishable. That's the whole point."

"Think with me. You are different and distinct from every other human being because your path on earth is like no other's. Where you have gone, when you have been there, is unique to you, and irreproducible. Even if someone tried to make themselves exactly like you, they'd fail in a thousand ways. They could never match your path on earth.

"Then, your path in life is solely yours. Your decisions, your dilemmas, desires, and responses. All of these are yours alone, and they are known perfectly and completely by God. No one else can respond to life exactly as you have done. No one ever will.

"Further, your time on earth is yours alone. Even if a million people shared your birthday, to the second, and your death, they will still be distinct and different from you because of the places they have been and the things they have done.

"It doesn't stop there. As you walk your path on the surface of the earth, in the precise time limits of your existence, your path in God's universe is completely and uniquely yours, and equally distinguishable to God. For one thing, you move about on the planet like no one else. Then, the earth is spinning from day to day, so that your location in the solar system is constantly circling. This circling path is made into a unique spiral by the concurrent revolving of earth around the sun. The pitch of this spiral is dependent on the seasons, the tilt of the earth on its axis. On top of that, our solar system is located in the galaxy, which itself is spinning through space, in a universe that is constantly expanding. Your universal path is a complex trajectory through space, made up of all these motions, simultaneously, and all God needs to have in order to identify you, and you alone, is one universal location at one particular point in time. Any particular point, at any particular time."

Sara whispered, "God's GPS."

"On an infinite scale, yes. God's GPS. And this is your identity, uniquely. It's as much who you are as your personality is. God charts the individual trajectories of every living thing. He knows his creation. He numbers the hairs of our heads."

Cal had said this all in a state of reverie, not really looking at Sara or Jeremiah, not actually noticing their reactions to his comments. When he looked up, finally, he saw that Sara was crying, and smiling intermittently, too. He leaned closer, took her hands into his, and said, "You alone are Sara. No one will ever be able to change that. To dress alike, and act alike, and live alike, as Amish, does not hold the power to diminish you. Not in my eyes. Not in God's."

MONDAY, AUGUST 2

29

ANDY STUTZMAN took a pull on a pint bottle of whiskey and climbed out of his car, parked behind the grocery store at tiny Becks Mills. He circled around to the front and keyed John Schlabaugh's unregistered cell phone to display the number of the last incoming call. At the public phone mounted on the front wall of the grocery store, he dialed the number and waited impatiently as it rang through.

It was Samuel White's voice that came back to him, "Yeah? What?"

Andy said, "I've got your Holmes County drugs and money in a briefcase. You want it back?"

"Who is this?"

"Never mind that, White. Do you want your drugs back or not? Maybe I'll just keep the money."

"I don't know who you are, pal, but you just bought yourself a world of hurt."

"You're wasting my time, White. I need an answer. Yes or no."

"OK, yes. What's the deal?"

"I'm just an Amish kid who needs to make a fast couple thousand. So I'm gonna keep some of your money. If you want the rest, you need to come out to Becks Mills."

"How am I gonna find that?"

"Knock it off, White. You've met Johnny Schlabaugh out here half a dozen times that I know of."

"When?"

"I'll give you an hour. Then I'm gonna disappear, and you can kiss your junk good-bye."

"I'll need a couple of hours, anyway."

"You're wasting my time, again, White. One hour. Becks Mills. Be there."

* * *

White pulled a late-model Toyota 4Runner onto the gravel lot in front of the Becks Mills grocery store and found a black Amish buggy waiting for him at the edge of the store's security lighting, with a young Amish man on the seat. White climbed out of the Toyota, palmed a small automatic handgun, and approached the buggy cautiously. Five feet off, in dim light, he brandished the weapon and said, "Either you've got what I want, or you're a dead man."

Sounding unimpressed, John Miller replied, "Give me a break, White. If you want your drugs and money, climb aboard."

White looked around slowly, scanning for danger, and moved cautiously to the edge of the buggy. He pointed the gun at Miller's head and climbed awkwardly up to the seat beside him. To Miller, he said, "I don't know what you think you're doing, but this isn't going to turn out how you planned."

Through the part in the black curtain separating the front of the buggy from the back, Andy Stutzman pointed the muzzle of a side-by-side, double-barreled shotgun at the back of White's head, saying, "I think a 12-gauge coach gun trumps a peashooter any day of the week, White."

White cursed and turned slowly to face the gun. Andy planted the muzzle behind White's freckled ear, pushed his head back around, and said, "Over your shoulder, now, White, hand that thing back to me."

White held his gun up to the side of John Miller's head and said, "How's about I just kill your friend here?"

Andy cocked both hammers on the coach gun and said, "You want to die, do you, White?"

"You're Amish. You're not gonna kill anyone."

"I've left home, White. I can never go back. Wouldn't live Amish now if I could."

"You're drunk, kid. I can smell it on your breath."

"Been drinking, yes. But drunk, no. And my trigger finger is as twitchy as a squirrel's tail. So I suggest you hand your gun back here, and we can get busy with the reason we're out here."

"OK, let's do it," White said, and handed over his gun.

"Next, White, so I know you won't pull a fast one, put your hands behind your back."

"Why?"

Andy poked the muzzle hard against the back of White's skull and snarled, "Do it!"

"Go screw yourself," White said, and started to turn in his seat.

Andy threw a rapid twist on the shotgun and clipped White behind the ear with the butt of the gun.

White groaned and slumped forward, and John Miller grabbed him by the shirtsleeve and held him upright. Andy laid the shotgun on the floorboards in the rear of the buggy, secured White's wrists behind his back with handcuffs, and hauled White by his shirt collar onto his back, in the rear of the buggy. He stepped over him, and climbed with his shotgun into the seat where White had been sitting. White, squirming sluggishly on his back, muttered, "You're dead. You got that? You're a dead man."

Andy said to John, "Let's get going."

As John pulled out onto the blacktop of Holmes County Road 19, a second buggy appeared from the surrounding darkness and took a position in front. A third buggy materialized and fell in behind John's rig. Andy's car appeared from the back of the grocery store and followed.

183

Andy took another tug on his whiskey bottle and shouted, "Up to the school, boys! We're almost done!"

* * *

When White fully regained consciousness, he was being hauled out of the back of the buggy in the dark at Gypsy Springs schoolhouse, just over the hill from Saltillo. Andy Stutzman had a hold of his arms, still shackled behind his back, and two Amish boys had his feet. As he cleared the buggy, Andy flipped him out into the gravel.

White hit the gravel face first, cursing, and Andy kicked him on the side of his head with the edge of his boot.

White spat out gravel and swore. To Andy he said, "You're a drunk, kid. You got your own friend killed, and for nothing. It's your own fault!"

Andy shouted "No!" and took a firm hold on White's belt. He rolled him forcefully onto this back, and hissed, "I'm gonna kill you." He planted a knee beside White's head and angrily knotted his fingers into a handful of red hair.

John Miller, dressed in traditional blue denim, stepped forward and laid a hand on Andy's shoulder. "This is not the way, Andy. This wasn't the plan. Nobody was supposed to get hurt."

Andy produced a folding knife, flipped out a long blade, and took the grip in his fist as if he were going to stab it down on White's neck. In the moonlight, the boys crowded closer and saw White's eyes bulging wide at the sight of the blade.

John Miller made a grab for Andy's arm, but Andy wrenched free of Miller's grasp and shouted, "He killed Johnny! Don't you understand? Johnny tried to save me. I've got to do this to square it with Johnny." He craned his neck to look up at Miller, shiny tears streaming tracks down his cheeks.

John leaned over and whispered in Andy's ear, "You're not going to involve us in a killing, Andy. We didn't bargain for this."

White protested, "You can't just . . ." and Andy cracked him across the nose with the butt of the knife.

One of the Amish boys backed up from White and Stutzman, shaking his head. The second took hold of John Miller's sleeve and pulled Miller back toward the buggies, saying, "Nicht recht, John. Nicht recht."

John slowly backed up a couple of paces and said, "It's not right, killing a man, Andy."

"What do you want from me, John? I'm the only one willing to face this punk. He killed Johnny! Don't you get that?"

"You're drunk, again," said Miller. "This is not our way."

"Do you really think you can live your entire life as a pacifist?"

"Why did White kill Johnny, Andy?"

"He is evil. That's reason enough for a guy like him."

"Jeremiah said that Abe saw you lunge at White."

"Don't say that! Don't you dare say that."

"What if you hadn't been the aggressor? What if you had not lunged at him?"

Groaning, "It's not my fault."

"Did you think you could stop him from beating Johnny? Did you think you had that power?"

"You weren't there. You'd have been useless."

"You're talking about murder, Andy! Murder plain and simple."

"Payback, John! It's just payback."

"It is wrong."

"I can't live Amish. My family won't even talk to me anymore."

"Even the English would say this is wrong."

"English know a little more about justice than Amish do."

"Justice is not ours to demand."

"It is!"

"No, Andy. We do not expect justice in this world."

"Name one thing, John, that would be better."

"Peace, Andy. Peace is better."

"Then I guess you're all ready for Amish beards. They've got you brainwashed."

"Your guilt about Johnny has blinded you to peace."

"I'm not guilty about anything. And I'm not a hypocrite, either, preaching about peace. The only reason Amish have peace to squawk about is because there are plenty of English people willing to fight to keep the peace. Hypocrites! Aren't willing to do anything about it for themselves. They let the English do it all. Do what is necessary so cowards can live in peace."

"I don't care what you think. You shouldn't have lunged at White, and it's tearing you up. And you shouldn't be planning to kill White now."

"Then you'd better all clear out. This English trash caused all our problems, and I'm going to do something about it for once."

"You're wrong, Andy. We did all this to ourselves. We wanted the drugs. We wanted the wild life. We left out homes to find the world. The guilt is ours."

"I didn't kill Johnny. White did that."

"Who even knew there was a Samuel White before Johnny went to Columbus for the drugs?"

"Are you saying it's Johnny's fault?"

"It's all our faults, Andy. Yours, mine, everyone's."

A sigh. "You'd better clear out of here, John. Just get out before it's too late."

John Miller motioned for the other Amish lads to leave. Two boys got into one of the buggies and drove up to the blacktop, disappearing with a clatter of hooves on pavement, into the dark. Ben Troyer stayed put. John stepped back a little from Andy and said, "Do you really think this will give you peace?"

"To hell with peace! I want justice."

"There can be no justice without peace."

"Like I said, you've been brainwashed."

"Amish know this truth of peace better than anybody."

"Then I'll settle for English justice, such as it is."

"If that's what you want, turn White over to Robertson."

"Get out, John, while you can."

"Turn him over to Robertson, Andy."

"I'm not going to argue anymore. It's all on me now."

"Then you wait until we clear out of here, Andy. You're on your own."

"So get out!" Andy growled. "Get out if you can't take it." He wiped tears from his eyes with his sleeve and jerked White's head off the ground, fingers knotted in his hair. He smashed White again in the face and glared at his friends. "Get out! Get out of here!"

"What about the stuff?" Miller asked from his buggy. "We all brought our gadgets, like you said. We thought this was going to be peaceful."

"Dump it all out on the ground," Andy whispered. "Just dump it all out and leave. I've got to do this, now. While I've still got the courage. It's all on me, John, from here on out. Tell the sheriff you were never here."

30

Monday, August 2
Dawn

PROFESSOR Branden sat before sunrise at the cliff's edge, at the back of the Brandens' lot, on their oak bench, sipping a mug of strong coffee. When dawn broke free over the eastern hills, the sun hung in the morning mist like a fuzzy peach, the valley below suffused with yellow and gold. It had become a habit for him that summer to enjoy the sunrise there with Caroline.

As he was finishing his coffee, Caroline came out to him in her bathrobe, carrying a carafe of fresh coffee. She had his cell phone, and she told him, as she sat down, that a message had beeped in while she was getting out of bed. Branden keyed in his codes and read two lines of numbers, GPS coordinates:

N 40° 31.318'
W 81° 51.288'

Latitude and longitude.

He showed the message to Caroline, and said, "This is out by Saltillo."

"That's all it is?" she asked. "Just the numbers?"

"That's all," he said and closed the phone. "Coordinates."

"Someone wants you to go there?"

"That's as good a guess as any."

Together, they rose, went inside, dressed in jeans and matching blue shirts, and drove Caroline's Miata down to the red brick jail at Courthouse Square. When they entered by the north door, they found Ellie Troyer behind her reception counter. Italian opera boomed through her wall from Bruce Robertson's office. A vibrant and confident soprano voice carried splendidly through the wall, and Ellie seemed unsure whether to smile or frown. In the next refrain, Robertson's brute bass voice picked up with the soprano, and mangled the harmonies. Despite his damage to the music, his enthusiasm offset his impact on the soprano's rich, expressive renderings. Ellie Troyer spread her arms and smiled, saying, "What can I say?"

"How long's he been like this?" Branden asked.

"Missy took him to a Sarah Brightman concert over the weekend," Ellie explained. "Now he's got some Italian language tapes so he can teach himself to understand the lyrics."

"That must have been some kind of concert," Caroline said.

Branden said, "Before this, his favorite music was cowboy songs about Wyoming and Montana."

"If you get him started in on this topic," Ellie said, "you're gonna be here a while."

Caroline touched the professor's arm and said, somewhat imploringly, "Maybe we don't need to bother him, Michael."

Branden said, "Ellie, we need to use the GPS receiver from the Schlabaugh case. Any chance of getting that, without interrupting Caruso in there?"

Ellie laughed, said, "Follow me," and led down the hall, past Robertson's office door. In the squad room, she keyed open a locker and took out a plastic crate marked "Schlabaugh." From the crate, she produced the GPS receiver, and locked everything else back in the locker.

Branden signed for the unit, giving his badge number, and drove out to the high ridge at Saltillo. With Caroline's help, he compared their location with the coordinates from the cell phone message. He looped around the triangle and turned west onto County 68.

After a quarter mile, they came to the lane that cut down from the blacktop to the Gypsy Springs schoolhouse. As they turned in, the figure of a tall, redheaded man was visible, his arms pinned back, his body strapped to the backstop of the softball diamond behind the school.

When they got down to the softball diamond, they found Samuel Red Dog White trussed and bound to a white upright pole of the backstop. His head was lifted high, and his windpipe rattled dangerously as he labored for breath. His neck was wound with several loops of a bungee cord, and the cord was hooked at both ends, on either side of his head, to the fencing of the backstop. It had a stranglehold on his larynx, and White couldn't talk. By the sound of it, he could barely breathe.

Caroline stood back, and the professor advanced to the edge of a pile of gadgets that had been stacked at White's feet. Branden leaned over, braced himself on the fencing, and unhooked one side of the bungee cord. He unhooked the other side, and released the tension on the cord. White retched and struggled for air. To his chest was pinned a note, printed in pen on wide-ruled grade-school paper: "So he will know what it was like for Sara."

Branden took a step back and toed several items in the pile at White's feet. Then he turned to Caroline and said, "It's OK. He can't move."

Caroline came up behind her husband and stared at the sign pinned to White's chest. She knelt and lifted an iPod music player from the pile at his feet. Her eyes carried questions, and Branden shrugged.

The professor opened his cell phone, called Robertson, and told the sheriff that he'd need to get out to Gypsy Springs School with a couple of deputies. Then he knelt and started sorting through the items that had been stacked on the ground, apparently as an offering.

There were two CD players and a scattering of music disks, mostly rock and roll, rap, or hip-hop. Three GPS receivers were wedged into the stack. Four cell phones. Pornography magazines and videos. Two boom boxes. A video camera and several video-tapes rubber-banded together. There was also a black revolver and a sawed-off shotgun. Boxes of ammunition. A small TV and two VCR players. A PDA. Computer disks. Whiskey bottles. And a video game box, all of it arranged on top of a knee-high pile of English clothes, belts, sport shirts, dress slacks, and loafers.

Branden stepped back and whistled in admiration.

Caroline asked, "What does it mean?"

Branden ruffled his brown hair and said, "It means that most of those kids have quit their Rumschpringe."

*　*　*

By the time Bruce Robertson had White cut down from the back-stop, word had spread. Buggy traffic increased on 68, people being as curious as they are. A group of a dozen onlookers on foot had gathered along the blacktop, and a few adventuresome youth had come down the slope of the schoolyard to have a closer look.

Bishop Raber cut his rig out of the procession, and came down the lane to the softball diamond. He parked to the side, and watched Ricky Niell push White's head down to deposit him in the backseat of a black-and-white cruiser. White's hands were cuffed behind him, and there was less room in the backseat than was com-fortable for a man of his size. When White tried to protest, Ricky slammed the door shut on him and walked away.

Bishop Raber walked slowly to the pile of English gadgets and clothes that had been stacked at White's feet. He stood for a long time, gazing with satisfaction on the symbolism of the offering.

Eventually, Professor Branden joined him. "Everything is there, just as we found it."

"Yes," Raber said, "it is over."

Bruce Robertson, in uniform, joined them and said, "All right with you, Bishop, if I just get rid of this stuff? Give some of it to Goodwill?"

Raber nodded. "We have no use for such things, Sheriff. I'll find out who did this, if you want me to."

Robertson stroked his chin, smiled, and said, "That won't be necessary."

The bishop left, urged his horse up the grade, and went about dispersing the crowd that had gathered on 68.

When the sheriff's photographer had finished with the scene, and everything had been catalogued, Niell drove White into town. A second cruiser followed with the gadgets and clothes.

Caroline had stepped aside while the deputies worked, and the sheriff and the professor found her sitting on the wooden steps of the schoolhouse.

As they came up, she said, "Is that going to be the end of it?"

Robertson took off his uniform hat and wiped out the sweat-band. He looked at the professor and said, "What do you think?"

Branden answered, "I think Tony Arnetto is going to be happy we got White."

Robertson said, "I'm not sure Arnetto is the happy type. At any rate, we know Samuel White killed John Schlabaugh."

"He also kidnapped Sara Yoder," Caroline said.

"He did, or his people did it for him," the professor said. "He also shot Abe Yoder."

"All the other kids are safe," Caroline said.

Up on the road, the last of the onlookers was headed back toward Saltillo. Dan Wilsher finished photographing tracks in the sandy ground of the softball diamond.

Branden said to Robertson, "You going to follow this up?" nodding his head at Wilsher.

Robertson said, "We're just being thorough."

"Any ideas how they pulled it off?" Branden asked.

"It's the phones," Robertson said. "They must have got him out here that way. From all the tracks, I'd say there were four or five of them, in buggies. And they had two weapons that we know of."

"Jeremiah Miller didn't use his cell phone," Branden said. "But he could have made calls from pay phones, and we'd never have known it."

"It doesn't matter," Robertson said. "I'm not going to follow it up. Some good citizen did us a favor, and that's enough for me. On this case, at any rate."

"So, what's left?" the professor asked.

"We've got a briefcase full of money and drugs," Robertson said, "and a revolver from the cabin where Abe Yoder was hiding. My guess is it will check out with ballistics. Amish boys don't shoot people."

"You've also got a red Pontiac," Branden said.

"Impounded," Robertson said. "I consider it confiscated. I don't think John Schlabaugh's family is going to argue with that."

"You closed down an Ecstasy lab and a score of dealers," Caroline said.

"That we did," Robertson said. "That we did."

"This all started out with nine kids," Branden said. "Have you ever seen anything so extreme before, Bruce?"

Robertson shook his head and put his hat back on. "Abe Yoder got off easy, considering he might have died."

"Of the six kids left from that gang," Branden said, "two have left the area. Mary Troyer up at Middlefield, and Henry Erb out to Kansas."

"That leaves four," Robertson said.

"Would four determined Amish fellas, like members of Schlabaugh's gang, be enough to trick and capture Samuel White?" Branden asked.

"I'm going to have to believe that they would," Robertson said. "I'm going to choose to believe that they did."

Caroline let a moment pass, then said, "I don't know about you two, but this surprises me. A lot. Whoever did this was extremely resourceful. I have a hard time holding Amish in mind, when thinking about this level of intensity. And I don't think you two are any different. I'm betting this one took you by surprise."

"We were never very far out in front," Robertson admitted.

The professor said, "I haven't had much time to think about it, really."

"Before this," Caroline asked, "did you think Amish kids could take things so far?"

"No," the professor said.

"Not in a million years," said Robertson.

"Then Sara Yoder is a very lucky girl," Caroline said. "Holmes County's finest detectives were just following hunches."

"I don't think it was that bad," Branden said, and laughed.

"I don't either," Robertson added.

"If you hadn't talked with Abe Yoder, you'd never have saved her."

"But we did talk to Abe Yoder," the professor offered.

"Still," Caroline said. "I don't know."

"We were lucky," Branden said.

Caroline tipped her head at the backstop where White had been pinned. "I'd say White was lucky, too, gentlemen. I'd say he was very lucky indeed."

THURSDAY,
AUGUST 12

31

Thursday, August 12
7:30 A.M.

MARTHA YODER stood behind Sara, seated in her upstairs bedroom, and brushed Sara's hair gently. "Your father's going to want
to talk with you before you go down," she said.

Sara nodded and turned around to face her mother. "Is he . . .
angry?"

"No, sweet child. No, not at all. I think he has a present for you."

"Hawe you . . . crying, Mother?"

"I puddle up from time to time."

"Jeremiah . . . good man. Be a good husband."

"I know."

"Then . . . what is it?"

"I wish you hadn't been so wild, Sara. I wish you hadn't gotten
hurt."

"Going to be . . . fine."

"Oh, Sara! You're so young."

"Older than you were. When you and Papa . . . married."

"That was different."

"Really? Are you sure?"

"I was never a wild child, Sara. I didn't have much of a Rumschpringe in my day."

"Just as well. Not all it's cracked . . . to be."

When she had put up her hair and finished dressing, Sara's two
youngest sisters, Annie, seven, and Lizzie, five, came into the bedroom. Annie gave her a picture she had done in crayon—a large

stick-figure girl in the upper left corner, with a small smudge of a little girl, either kneeling or sitting, in the lower left corner under a tree with a scribble of green leaves and a thick brown trunk. Lizzie gave her a bundle of wildflowers she had picked that morning.

Annie asked, in a small, high voice, "Are you going to visit us, Sara?" She sounded worried.

Sara leaned over, scooped the girls into her arms, and held them close for a long time. Then she said, eyes moist with tears, "You'd better believe it."

"Are you going to have babies now?" asked Lizzie.

"If I can, Lizzie. If I can."

"Are you Amish now?" Lizzie asked shyly.

"Yes, little one. I . . . Amish."

When the girls had left, Albert O. Yoder came in bashfully and said, "You ready to do this, Sara? Are you sure?"

Sara said, "Yes, Papa. Jeremiah's . . . good . . . man."

"Those Millers are a frugal bunch."

"Be fine, Papa."

"If you ever need anything, you ask your husband first, and then you come see me."

Sara nodded and smiled.

"I've picked out a breeding pair of goats for you. At least you'll have milk."

"Be fine, Papa. You . . . stop worrying."

"Oh, you're sure of that, are you, Sara?"

"I am."

"A father never stops worrying. From the day you were born, until the day I die."

*   *   *

Sara Yoder didn't care that, in many obvious and telling ways, her wedding was not traditional. She knew there would be endless gossip over this within her family, near and far, and among her neighbors. But Sara didn't mind. To her it mattered only that she was able to spend her day on crutches, not in a wheelchair, and that, when asked her vows, she would be able to reply with a strong and confident "Yes." Yes to Jeremiah Miller. Yes to marriage. Yes to the church.

She had talked at length with her parents about the details. Sara's would be a rare summer wedding, a departure from the usual practice of holding weddings in the fall or winter, after the harvest. Hers would be a small gathering, by Amish standards. Usually, all of the bride's relatives and neighbors would be invited and would be expected to attend. For Sara's relatives, scattered through Indiana, Michigan, and Wisconsin, a journey during the growing season would be burdensome and impractical. A summer wedding posed less of a problem for Jeremiah, since invitations are traditionally extended only to the groom's immediate family.

Following local tradition, the wedding ceremony was to take place not at the bride's house but at the Albert P. and Miriam Yoder residence down the lane. After the ceremony at the neighbors' house, the bride's family would then be responsible for all the food and preparations at their own house. By tradition, the religious service, ceremony, and fellowship would last the entire day. It was to be a Thursday wedding, according with the tradition that weddings be held on either a Tuesday or a Thursday.

Sara and Jeremiah stood up to be married with four witnesses or attendants, called *nevvehocker*. Sara had chosen two of her cousins as attendants, and Jeremiah, two of his uncles. The four witnesses were dressed like the bride and groom, so that to the unknowing, it would not be obvious, until the ceremony began, who among them would be married. This is a tradition held over from the years of European persecution.

Jeremiah and his two *nevvehocker* wore homemade blue serge suits and collarless white shirts of cotton broadcloth. Sara wore a light blue cotton dress with a high neckline, a full-length skirt with a white organdy kerchief in a pocket, and a matching apron reaching from her neck to the hem of her skirt. Her prayer cap was white.

The ceremony at the neighbors' house started traditionally, with a two-hour hymn service, the men sitting separate from the women. Then followed two hours of preaching on weddings in the Bible. Sara and Jeremiah had picked their two favorite preachers for this duty, and they had asked Cal Troyer to conclude with the traditional story from the Old Testament about the wedding of Tobias.

Before their vows were spoken, Sara and Jeremiah met with Bishop Raber upstairs for the *Vermahnung*, their final instructions and exhortations from the bishop about married life.

The actual rites, later in the morning, proceeded in German. Sara's voice was confident, but still somewhat impaired.

Friends and family were seated on the lawn behind the wedding party. The bishop started without formalities, saying, "Do you recognize it as a Christian Order that there should be one man and one woman, and can you hope too that you have started this union according to the Christian Order?

Sara looked at Jeremiah, and he at her, and together they answered, "Yes."

The bishop continued. "Can you too hope, Brother, that the Lord might have ordained this our Sister as a married wife?"

Jeremiah smiled, glanced at his uncles behind him and loudly stated, "Yes."

To Sara, the bishop likewise said, "Can you too hope, Sister, that the Lord might have ordained this our Brother as a married husband?"

Sara nodded, paused to focus on her word, and said, "Yes."

The bishop drew himself up a little straighter and looked over the audience. He turned his gaze to Jeremiah and said, "Do you promise to your married wife that if she should come into bodily weakness, sickness, or any kind of condition, that you will care for her as is becoming a married Christian man?"

Jeremiah answered, "Yes."

To Sara, the bishop said, likewise, "Do you promise to your married husband that if he should come into bodily weakness, sickness, or any kind of condition, that you will care for him as is becoming a married Christian woman?"

Sara smiled and answered, "Yes."

A little louder, now, the bishop said, "Do you both also promise to the Lord and to the community that you will bear with each other love, life, and patience, and not separate from one another until the dear Lord will part you through death?"

Sara and Jeremiah answered yes, and managed, both, to relax slightly.

The bishop concluded: "So we see that Raguel took the hand of the daughter and put it into the hand of Tobias and said, 'The God of Abraham, the God of Jakob, the God of Isaac be with you and help you together, and give you his blessing richly over you,' and all this through Jesus Christ. Amen."

FRIDAY, AUGUST 13

32

Friday, August 13
6:50 A.M.

CAROLINE was up before the professor and waited for him in her pajamas, with a carafe of coffee, on their oak bench with a view of the Amish valley and the hills east of Millersburg. When he came out to join her, he was already dressed in work boots, old jeans, a heavy work shirt with long sleeves, and a Cleveland Indians ball cap.

Caroline looked him over and shook her head, as if he were the worst variety of scoundrel. She poured his coffee and set it on the bench beside her, saying, "What can be more important than our mornings together, Michael?"

He sat beside her, took up his mug, and said, "There's no hurry. I predict, however, that you'll find this little adventure to be worth every second we put into it."

She sipped at her coffee wordlessly for several minutes, enjoying the peaceful view off the cliffs at the back of their lot. Eventually, she asked, "What gives, Professor?"

"Oh, nothing, really. I thought we might make a little trip in the truck."

"Will I need to dress like a sodbuster?" she said, laughing at his attire.

"Work clothes would be appropriate," he answered.

Protesting the interruption of her morning, Caroline got dressed as suggested and found her husband in the garage, loading gear into his short bed truck. Caroline watched, amused, as he stowed two large flashlights, a length of strong rope, a Coleman lantern, a heavy tarp, a pry bar, and a bottle of champagne in an ice bucket. She got in on the passenger's side, and he drove without explanation or comment to the house of the late Spits Wallace.

At the back door, he clipped the yellow police tape and unlocked the door to the kitchen. While she waited there, he went back to the truck and brought the two flashlights, the Coleman lantern, the pry bar, and the bottle of champagne in a backpack slung over his shoulder. He handed her one of the flashlights and led the way down to the basement.

Once there, he said, while studying the concrete block walls, "Two things have bothered me about the Spits Wallace affair. One, how did he disappear so handily that afternoon when Samuel White came knocking on his door? Two, why didn't we find any gold?"

Caroline stood in the middle of the dank basement and watched him skeptically as he traced the electric wires in the basement. After several minutes, he fingered one line and followed it to a small hole between the top of the concrete blocks and the framing joist of the house. He lit a match and held it near the hole through which the wire passed. The flame blew out. He lit another match. Again, it blew out.

Smiling, he lit the Coleman lantern and began to study the grouting between the blocks. Soon he had marked off a narrow rectangle. He wedged his pry bar into one of the seams, and the rectangle pivoted toward him as if it were on hinges.

What he had discovered was a small wooden door, fronted by a thin layer of fake blocks, leading to a crouching tunnel. With a smile, he stooped, entered the tunnel, and held the lantern so that Caroline could follow. Inside, there was an electric switch and a string of lights down the tunnel. The professor turned them on.

In the yellow glow of the string of light bulbs, the tunnel led slowly and gently down for about a hundred feet and terminated in a small cave. Branden shined his flashlight upward, and they saw overhead, fallen partway into the cavern, the tumbled logs of the decrepit old cabin that sat on the Wallace property.

An opening to their left widened to a larger cavern with a steep, rocky slope. They carefully helped each other negotiate the slope, and came out on a flat underground table of rock. There they found an old blanket, a rusty shotgun, a kerosene lantern, and cans of food. And in the corner, there was a large stack of canvas moneybags.

The professor opened one and pulled out a handful of heavy gold coins, dating from the nineteenth century. Astonished despite his earlier reckonings, he knelt beside the pile of coin bags and started to laugh.

Caroline said, laughing too, "This is the famous Wallace coin collection?"

Unable to reply verbally, the professor nodded in the affirmative.

"What made you think it was here?" Caroline asked, and took one of the coins to admire it in the white light of the hissing Coleman lantern.

"He was too dirty," the professor said. "Both times we saw him he was covered with dirt and mud. And I knew he had his daddy's coins, despite what he said."

"You noticed his dirty clothes?"

"That's it, really. I figured he had been working in a tunnel or a cave, and then I remembered he said he made himself scarce when Samuel White came up his drive."

As astonished with him as she had ever been, Caroline said, "What are we going to do with it?"

The professor grinned at her like a grade-schooler who had caught his first snake.

Caroline exclaimed, "You wouldn't dare!"

The professor said, "I never told you much about Spits Wallace and me. Spits Wallace has few relatives. His wife and parents are all dead. He had no children. No brothers or sisters. And, here sits his gold."

Caroline cautiously repeated, "What are you going to do with it, Michael?"

"Spits Wallace's father was old Earl Wallace. And old Earl didn't trust the banks. But I got to know him pretty well, and he showed me once where he had rigged up booby traps for anyone who might try to steal his gold."

"Seems like a strange connection for a college professor," Caroline said.

"When I was a kid, my dad used to bring me along to visit old Earl. He kept trying to sell Wallace insurance on his gold coin collection. I'd play with little William."

"You may be the only person alive who knew Spits Wallace's given name."

"Could be."

"So you knew his father from those trips with your dad."

"That, yes, but after my parents were killed, my lawyer got me involved with his old man. I was in college and pretty sour, I guess, so he thought it would do me some good to meet this guy. Henry DiSalvo was the lawyer. Anyway, Henry told me to come along on a call with him. Out to the Wallace place. Earl Wallace was dying of lung cancer, and DiSalvo was his lawyer, too. Henry thought it'd be good for me to meet Earl, and in a strange way it was. I came out here every other day or so that summer, and I got to know the old man pretty well. William, Spits, was living with his mother then, in Youngstown, and I'd sit and talk with Earl for hours. That's when I learned about his coin collection and the booby traps he had set up to protect it. He was a hardscrabble porcupine of an old goat, but I liked him. My grandfather had known him growing up, and they both belonged to the muzzle-loader club back then. Earl could hit a walnut at a hundred paces. Long story short, he died that summer, and William moved back home."

"How is this related to anything now, Michael?"

"Old man Earl didn't like his son. Didn't like people in general, but didn't like his son in particular. Said his son was too much like his mother. He used to say that his son wasn't good enough for all his gold. None of his relatives was good enough. 'Ain't any dang fool gonna get my gold.' Said that more than a few times.

"Gold was the only thing he liked. It took him a lifetime to collect it all. Started buying and trading gold coins while he was still a teenager, back when gold hadn't shot up like it did. He got hooked on it, and started selling off household goods to buy more coins. Spent all his savings and spent all of his wife's savings, too. He didn't care that he lived in a shack and drove a rusty pickup. Spent every dime he made on coins. His obsession with gold cost him everything he had. It's why his wife eventually left him. But Earl didn't care about her by then at all. He settled up with her in the divorce by selling off some of his collection, but her lawyers never really knew how much he had, so I suspect he got off easy. I'd sit with him on his old porch, and he'd talk for hours about how he wished he had never met the woman. Other days it'd be the other way around. He'd reminisce about their younger years, when he had first met her. What a looker she had been. Wondering what went wrong.

"And he felt guilty for some reason about the way Spits turned out. Earl had been too hard raising the boy, and something had happened between them. So, he didn't like Spits at all, but he also couldn't just cut him out of his will altogether. He wasn't willing to disown him outright. Anyway, Earl wrote out a will and left his gold to his son. Didn't like the idea, really, but we talked it through, and old Earl came to accept the idea that it was the right thing to do."

"You're not really getting to the point, Michael."

The professor gave a satisfied smile and a bemused shake of his head. In the harsh light of the Coleman lantern, he popped the cork on the champagne bottle. The cork thudded against the rock ceiling of the cave, and the champagne foamed out over the lip of the bottle. The professor held the bottle at arm's length to let the foam spill out onto the floor of the cave, and then he poured a glass for Caroline and one for himself.

"The point is, Caroline, unlike his father, Spits Wallace never wrote a will. So I've had Henry DiSalvo checking on who his closest blood relatives are. The people who will inherit this gold."

"Anyone we know?"

"Rabers, for the most part. About thirteen Rabers. There are a few distant relatives on his father's side, but Spits Wallace's mother was Bishop Irvin Raber's oldest sister. She took up with young Earl Wallace in her first year of the Rumschpringe and never went back to Amish ways."

"Sara made the right choice, didn't she, Michael?"

"She did indeed," said the professor, smiling, and clinked his glass to Caroline's.